THE ULTIMATE HOOD BETRAYAL

WRITTEN BY:

NATIONAL BESTSELLING AUTHOR,

PATRICE BALARK

The Ultimate Hood Betrayal

Copyright © 2020 by Patrice Balark

All rights reserved.

Published in the United States of America.

All rights reserved. No part of this publication may be reproduced, distributed, or transmitted in any form or by any means, including photocopying, recording, or other electronic or mechanical methods, without the prior written permission of the publisher, except in the case of brief quotations embodied in critical reviews and certain other noncommercial uses permitted by copyright law. For permission requests, please contact: www.authortwylat.com.

This is a work of fiction. Names, characters, places, and incidents either are the products of the author's imagination or are used fictitiously. Any resemblance of actual persons, living or dead, businesses, companies, events, or locales is entirely coincidental. The publisher does not have any control and does not assume any responsibility for author or third-party websites or their content.

The unauthorized reproduction or distribution of this copyrighted work is a crime punishable by law. No part of the e-book may be scanned, uploaded to or downloaded from file sharing sites, or distributed in any other way via the Internet or any other means, electronic, or print, without the publisher's permission. Criminal copyright infringement, including infringement without monetary gain, is investigated by the FBI and is punishable by up to five years in federal prison and a fine of $250,000 (www.fbi.gov/ipr/).

This e-book is licensed for your personal enjoyment only. Thank you for respecting the author's work.

Published by Twyla T. Presents, LLC.

EDITOR

Edited by Red Diamond Editing by V. Rena

reddiamondediting5@yahoo.com

CHAPTER ONE

"Dallas, your husband is here."

Looking up from her MacBook Pro, Dallas smiled at her receptionist Zarkia before standing to her feet.

"Tell that nigga I'm gone." She replied, rolling her eyes to the back of her head.

"I tried, but he drove through the alley already and seen your car in the back. He would have been back here already, but I told him that you were on a very important conference call, but the nigga getting impatient now." Zarkia reported before turning on her heels, heading back out the door.

Smacking her lips, Dallas fixed her silk Versace blouse and black H&M pencil skirt before walking around the cherry oakwood desk. Grabbing her black Chanel purse, she checked around the office one last time before cutting off the lights. Making sure the doorknob was locked, Dallas peeked out around the corner before slowly closing the door behind her.

Tiptoeing in her Christian Louboutin pumps, Dallas headed to the backdoor, thinking she could slip out while Chinks stood posted at the front door of her shop. Slowly unlocking the locks to the backdoor, Dallas opened it cautiously, praying that the alarm was not set. Pulling it open wider, Dallas thanked the petty gods that no sirens went off. Looking back one last time, she smiled to herself before yet another successful escape.

"Getcho dumb ass back in there." Vonte, Chinks' best friend said, pushing Dallas back inside her establishment.

Pissed to captivity, Dallas stubbornly didn't move, causing Vonte to use more force as he escorted her to the front of the shop.

"Let me the fuck go…. witcho pussy ass." Dallas snapped, fixing her clothes before walking ahead of him.

Emerging from the back, Dallas locked eyes with Zarkia first, who laughed from her spot behind the receptionist's desk. Mouthing the word "bitch" to her, she then directed her attention to her husband, who stood there looking at her.

"Her silly ass was trying to slip out the back bro." Vonte laughed, walking away from her as Dallas pushed him in the back.

"FUCK YOU!" she yelled out in the empty shop; her middle finger raised high in the air.

Irritated beyond repair, Dallas flipped her long jet-black weave out of her face before shifting her weight to one side. Her eyes still zoomed in on Chinks. Dallas waited to see what he had up his sleeve next, before she put him out. Slowly walking over towards where she was standing, Chinks cut his eyes at Vonte first before addressing his wife.

"Aye, I'll holler at you later bro."

"You…. getcho goofass in the back." Chinks demanded, pointing his finger towards the back office as Dallas stormed off.

Removing her keys from her purse, she unlocked the door and hit the lights while Chinks closed the door behind them. Walking over to her desk, Dallas slammed her purse down before turning around, facing her husband of five years.

"Why are you here?" she asked him, folding her arms across her chest as she leaned back against the desk.

Dallas watched Chinks lick his lips before slowly walking over towards her with a smirk on his face.

"Why you always mad over dumb shit baby?" he asked calmly, twisting his head to the side, trying to reason with her.

"DUMB SHIT CHINKS? ARE----YOU----SERIOUS?" She snapped, clapping her hands in between each word as she walked around him in a circle.

Standing in one spot, Chinks waited until she was done before he grabbed her by both arms, forcing her to focus on him.

"Look, I was wrong. I shouldn't have lied, but I did and now it's over with." He spoke, releasing her before going inside his pocket, retrieving his ringing phone.

Dallas stood there quietly, allowing his words to soak in her head as he ignored whoever was on the other end of the call.

"My problem is……" she started off by saying but was interrupted again.

"JUST ANSWER THE FUCKING PHONE CHINKS!" Dallas yelled just as his line began to ring a second time.

Looking over at her but not saying a word, Chinks did as she requested and answered his phone.

"YO!" a deep voice loudly spoke from the other end.

"Aye bro, I'm talking to my wife, let me hit you back." Chinks said, ending the call before the caller could reply.

"You happy Dallas? Now can we get back to the reason why I came here?" he pleaded with her as he put his phone away.

Stubbornly folding her arms across her chest, Dallas waited for Chinks to explain the reason for his visit. She had done so well dodging him for the day, and if it wasn't for the shop needing supplies, she would be checking in at a hotel or something.

"Why haven't you been answering yo phone all day?" he asked calmly, taking a seat on the edge of her desk.

"You asking questions? I thought you were explaining the reason you here." She reminded him, walking behind her desk and taking a seat in the leather black chair.

Letting out a long sigh, Dallas watched as Chinks rubbed his hands over his full beard. She knew that she was pissing him off and those were her exact intentions.

"Aight look, I went out with Vonte last night to Club Traverse. You know my homie Trell from over East birthday today and …."

"And what the fuck does that have to do with the price of tea in China? I wanna know why the fuck was Kinisha in yo face Chinks?" Dallas jumped up and asked, her anger growing by the second.

"If you shut the fuck up and listen, I'll get to that part." He barked, his tone matching hers precisely.

"You'll get to that part? I don't care to hear about all the bullshit prior. What I wanna know is, why the fuck was my husband in his ex-face? You can save everything else."

` Dallas took Chinks' silence as a way to buy time to think of a lie; when in fact, there was nothing he could say to justify his actions. So instead of him lying, Dallas spoke up first, putting everything on the table.

"I don't get it, but like I told you before, if you wanna be with that bitch, then I'll gladly sign those papers." Dallas continued, this time walking around from the desk, standing in front of him.

"Here you go with this bullshit man. I'll see you at home." Chinks dismissingly said, turning to leave but was stopped before he could make it to the door.

Running from the spot she was in, Dallas jumped in front of him, halting all movement, forcing him to stay.

"Where the fuck you think you going? This ain't no *"To Be Continued"* conversation, nigga. You must really think I won't leave you?" She spazzed, meaning each and every word.

"Baby, listen to me. I had no clue Kinisha was gon' be there and…"

"And when you seen her, you should have avoided her at all cost, but noooo, you wanna slap ass and get lap dances and shit." Dallas snapped, punching Chinks in the chest as hard as she could with a closed fist.

Unfazed by the love tap, Dallas looked up at her husband, who towered over her at six feet even. She loved Chinks with everything in her, but she refused to be one of those silly bitches who stuck with a nigga just because of the weight his name holds.

"Baby listen, I was at a club, its dancing, the shit innocent." He paused, staring deep into her hazel eyes before finishing his statement.

"What you need to do is stop listening to your miserable ass friends. All those hoes hating, and if one of dem bald-headed ass bitches hadn't sent you the video, we wouldn't be even having this conversation."

"So, let me get this right, had *MY* friends not sent me those videos, we wouldn't be having this conversation, right? So, fuck the fact that *you* shouldn't have been doing what *you* were doing? It's they fault, they shouldn't have shown me? I mean, Marquis, make it make sense."

Chinks' beady eyes stared at Dallas who stood her ground, ready for whatever bullshit response that he had next. Out of the five years that they had been married, this had been their biggest issue and ongoing problem.

"That's not what I'm saying…."

"What are you saying then? Because from where I'm standing, it sounds like you are trying to justify your actions by blaming it on my friends, which is not gon' fly. I put up with a lot of shit in this marriage but being blandly disrespected is not gon' be one. You need to decide what you gon' do before I decide for you. Now if you don't mind…. I have a shop to run."

Looking down at the gold Rolex on her arm, Dallas noticed it was ten minutes after three and time to open.

With Saturday always being the busiest day, Dallas needed to focus on the needs of her customers and not Chinks possible infidelities.

"Like I said, we'll finish this at home. I love you. See you later." Chinks finally replied, placing a kiss on Dallas's forehead before walking out of her office.

Following close behind on his heels, Dallas appeared from the back with her husband and smiled at the sight before her. "*Queenz Tatt*" had only been open fifteen minutes and there was already a crowd at the door.

"Boss Lady, what's good? How you been Chinks?" Monet, one of the tattoo artists, asked as they scrolled past her station.

The couple spoke to her in unison before heading towards the front door. After looking over the walk-in list on the clipboard, Dallas made brief eye contact with Zarkia before joining her husband outside.

"Do you know how late you'll be?" Chinks asked her, leaning back against the brick wall, pulling an already rolled blunt from behind his ear.

"Don't light that shit in front of my shop, but nah, I'm not sure. I'm going out with Neysa and Shonnie later, why?" she asked, shooting him a look out the side of her eye.

Dallas knew that whenever Chinks questioned her, he had something up his sleeve; rather it was dealing with hoes, money, or clothes, it was always something.

"Nah, I was just asking cuz I wanted you to slide through to Trell's party tonight at…."

"But I thought Trell had a party last night?" Dallas cut him off in mid-sentence and contested.

"He did, but today is his *actual* birthday Inspector Gadget…. but DAMN! Y'all gon' slide through or what?" Chinks asked, pulling a lighter from his pocket, sparking up the blunt.

Dallas wasn't a fan of Trell but seeing how her and her girls didn't have any other official plans, she decided to roll with it. It had been a few months since Dallas had fun, and what better way to bring in her hot girl summer than doing bald-head hoe shit with her friends?

CHAPTER TWO

"Dr. Brown, I have those lab orders that you requested. I placed them in the patient's chart for you whenever you are ready."

"Thanks so much Kelly, let Dr. Oxford know… I'm gone for the day." Neysa replied, flying out of the Pediatrics department at Oak Park hospital.

After working six sixteen-hour shifts, back to back, she was beyond tired and ready to start her month-long vacation. Hitting the locks on her candy apple red Range Rover, Neysa powerwalked through the parking lot, dropping her iPhone in the process.

"FUCK!" she cursed, slowly flipping the phone over, praying that she hadn't cracked her screen.

After silently thanking the man above, Neysa continued her strut to her car, getting inside and immediately rolling down the windows. It was June, the beginning of summer, but it felt like mid-August, the temperature in her truck read ninety-three degrees. Cranking up the engine, Neysa slowly pulled out of the parking spot, heading home to finally get some rest.

It was a little after four in the evening and Saturday traffic was good to her. Making it home under thirty minutes, Neysa parked her truck behind Ocean's Benz and got out. Picking up a flyer laying in her lawn, she read over the contents regarding a block party before balling up the piece of paper. Securing her Nike bookbag on her shoulders, Neysa headed up the stairs to the two-story home she proudly owned.

"This nigga must have the AC on fifty…. It's too fuckn' cold in here." She mumbled under her breath, heading to the thermostat that rested on the wall.

After adjusting the temperature, Neysa followed the voice of Nipsey Hussle to the basement, where she found Ocean sitting on the couch with a blunt in his mouth.

Last time that I checked

It was five chains on my neck

It was no smut on my rep, last time that I checked

I was sellin' zones in the set

Make a quarter mill no sweat, last time that I checked

I'm the street's voice out west

Glancing over at the tv, Neysa smiled at the sight of the late great rapper before walking over to the table and grabbing the remote.

"Wat's up baby?" Ocean said, releasing huge smoke circles in the air as Neysa turned the volume down on the tv.

"Hey baby! What's good?" she replied, flopping down next to him, immediately sliding out the Sketchers she worked in.

"Shittttt.... Chilling until later. How was work?" he questioned, dumping the ashes in the ashtray before handing the blunt to Neysa.

Grabbing the Swisher with her freshly manicured nails, Neysa hit it, inhaling the smoke before titling her head back on the couch.

"Two Medical Assistants called off, leaving me and my nurse to do EVERY FUCKING THING!" she yelled out in frustration before releasing the smoke through her nose.

"But the good news is.... I just paid the last payment on my student loans. I am officially out of debt." She continued, rejoicing the moment while taking another hard pull from the blunt.

"That's what's up, baby. We gon' celebrate tomorrow.... Imma put sum together fa ya." Ocean yawned, standing to his feet and stretching.

Looking up at him from her spot on the couch, Neysa's pussy jumped at the sight of his six-three, three-hundred-pound body. Neysa's eyes traveled from his bearded face down to his fat yet solid stomach, eventually stopping on thc bulge in his Adidas sweats.

"Why we gotta wait till tomorrow? Let's go out tonight and do something." She replied, reaching forward, rubbing his soft dick through his sweats.

"Can't…. Trell's party tonight and…."

"Ocean, didn't y'all just do something last night?" Neysa cut him off and replied as she felt an attitude approaching.

Snatching her hand away, she too stood up, her face colliding with his chest. She didn't have an issue with Ocean and him hanging with his friends, but it had been a while since they spent time alone.

"True, we kicked it last night and…."

"And y'all had a bunch of hoes in y'all section, including Kinisha and her whack weave wearing ass friends."

Neysa thought back to the call she received that morning from her best friend Dallas. Apparently, her husband Chinks was showing his ass in the club, and if Neysa knew any better, Ocean wasn't too far behind.

"So, I had Dallas forward me the video and just like I expected, you were on there…."

"I wasn't on there doing shit, Neysa…. shut the fuck up!" Ocean barked, walking away, leaving her standing there with her thoughts.

Pissed was an understatement, and honestly, Neysa wasn't done talking. Ocean was horrible at communicating, and the way he avoided his issues was by walking away, but today, that wasn't going to work.

"OCEAN…. OCEAN!" She yelled out, storming off and up the basement stairs.

"OCEAN… I KNOW YOU HEAR M…."

Neysa's words were cut off by the sound of the front door slamming. Running over bare feet to the window, Neysa watched as Ocean entered and disappeared in their garage. She thought about going out there, but the migraine that was building in the back of her head halted those actions. Instead, she went back downstairs to grab her phone before retreating to the bedroom.

Dropping her work bag at the door, Neysa placed her phone on the charger before heading into the bathroom.

Cutting on the shower, Neysa tested the water with her hands before taking off the navy-blue smock her wore.

Standing there naked, she began to critique her body in the mirror. Thoughts of plastic surgery plagued her mind as she imagined bigger breasts and a fatter ass. Neysa had what you called a "normal shape." She wasn't skinny nor was she fat. Her ass wasn't huge nor was it flat. Her breasts were her favorite asset, but she wouldn't mind her D-Cups being a little more perky. As bad as she contemplated surgery, she knew the risks, especially being in the medical field herself.

Tossing the idea to the back of her head, Neysa grabbed a face towel, checking the water temperature one last time before stepping in with one foot.

"AYE, YO PHONE RINIGING!" Neysa heard Ocean yell out over the water.

Taking her left foot out and closing the shower curtains shut, Neysa grabbed the pink and cream dry towel from behind the door before exiting the bathroom.

"Who is it? My momma?" she quizzed, eyeing him as she glided across the room to the nightstand.

"Nah, I'm not even sure, I didn't look." He replied, pulling out clothes from the top drawer.

Wondering in her mind about where he was headed, Neysa decided not to ask; instead, she grabbed her phone, returning Dallas's missed Facetime call.

"Hey friend." She beamed as soon as the call connected.

"Ewwww hoe, is you naked?" Dallas twisted up her face and asked, causing Neysa to laugh.

"Yes, I am. About to hop in the shower. What's up?" she replied, reentering the bathroom, closing the door behind her.

"Nothing really. I called to see if you wanted to crash Trell's party with me tonight?" Dallas inquired, causing Neysa's antennas to rise.

"Crash? Bitch, we damn near thirty…." Neysa said, pausing to take off her towel.

"What time you want me to be ready?" she continued, causing Dallas to burst out in laughter.

Propping the phone up on the sink, Neysa stepped inside the shower as if her best friend wasn't staring directly at her.

"But nah for real, Chinks asked me to come…."

"DAMN FOR REAL!" Neysa yelled over the running water as she lathered up her sponge.

"Girl yeah, he calls himself showing me that he's not on bullshit, but the damage was done last night. He claims it was just dancing, but… you know how that go." Dallas explained as Neysa washed her body for a second time.

"Don't trip friend. For all we know, it was just dancing…. Chinks ain't stupid." She said, consoling her friend but meaning every word.

That was the dope thing about Dallas and Chinks' marriage, they were best friends before anything. They had what people referred to as "relationship goals" and Neysa admired how happy he made her friend.

"He better not be stupid, but I'm still at the shop, I'll call you when I leave here." Dallas finally replied after a few seconds of silence, following Neysa's last statement.

"Say less. I'm about to sit on Ocean's face and then take a nap. Call me when you leave Queenz so we can turn up." Neysa said before stepping out of the shower, assuring that she kept her word.

CHAPTER THREE

Ayy

Trips that you plan for the next whole week

Bands too long for a nigga so cheap

And your flex OD, and your sex OD

You got it, girl, you got it (ayy)

You got it, girl, you got (yeah)

Pretty lil' thing, you got a bag and now you wildin'

As bad as Trinity wanted to sit this one out, her inter-hood rat wouldn't allow her to miss the first party of the summer. She had been back in Chicago for three-months, and after finally settling in at her new condo, Trinity was ready to let her hair down and enjoy the night.

Rubbing the lotion on her long legs, Trini sang along to Chris Brown and Drake's latest hit, "No Guidance." With the song on repeat, Trinity moved her body to the beat while the light skin duo serenaded her. The lyrics spoke to her as they rapped about a bad bitch, something she could definitely relate to.

You got it, girl, you got it

You got it, girl, you got it

Noticing her phone lightening up on the dresser, Trinity sat the lotion down on the bed before heading over to view the notification.

Shonnie: I thinkkkkkkk, I'm outside. I'm in front of a Silver Jag.

Smiling at the phone, Trinity shot her a text back, letting her know she was on her way out. Spraying on her favorite Gucci perfume, Trinity went inside the closet and grabbed the Giuseppe shoe box off the top shelf. Removing the black peep-toe boot, she slid on her shoes before checking her reflection in the mirror.

"Damn Ms. Howard," she cockily smirked, twirling around as she checked herself out from every angle.

Snatching up her designer clutch, Trinity did a mental checklist before cutting off the lights and locking up. Stepping out into the moonlight, she checked her surroundings before heading towards Shonnie's running car.

"OH MY GOD! LOOK AT YOUUUU1!!" Shonnie screamed as soon as Trinity opened the car doors.

"BITCH GET OUT! GIVE ME A HUG!" Trinity screamed, tossing her clutch on the passenger's seat before rushing around the car.

"You look amazing." The girls said in unison as they hugged.

"Atlanta has been good to you, I see." Shonnie said to her, releasing their embrace.

"And bitch you still ain't missed a beat." Trinity shot back, admiring how wonderful her high school best friend looked.

Walking back around to her side of the car, Trinity got in, a huge smile still plastered on her face. It felt good to be back home, and it felt even better knowing that her and her bestie was reunited for good.

"How long has it been? I feel like a horrible friend. You been back almost three months and I'm just now seeing you." Shonnie pouted, pulling away from Trinity's home.

"Girl, shut up. We both been busy. With you being this huge make-up artist to the stars and me hustling at the law firm.... Neither of us had time." Trinity replied, pulling down the sun visor, checking her lipstick.

Shonnie traveled for a living doing makeup, which is the reason why they hadn't spent time together sooner. Trinity was so busy settling in and working long hours at the law firm, she was too burned out to have fun.

"Speaking of hustling at the law firm, how's that going?" Shonnie glanced over at her and asked before emerging on the expressway.

"As much work as I do, I should be partner. Who knew making this transition from one state to another would be this stressful?" Trinity replied, shaking her head from side to side.

"I know friend, I just wish you'll go ahead and take the bar. The shit you do as a paralegal, you can be doing as a lawyer, making the amount of money that you really deserve." Shonnie preached the same as she did time after time.

"I see you over there rolling yo eyes, and I'm pretty sure that you tired of me saying this BUT…. you'll make a dope ass lawyer. Stop selling yourself short." Shonnie continued, causing Trinity to smile.

It was one thing, having these types of talks over the phone miles away, but being in the physical presence of that type of support was exactly what Trinity needed. Things such as that, let her know that moving back was the best decision ever.

"Sooooooo…. Trell's party! You ready?" Trinity looked down in her phone and asked, changing the subject to match the mood she was in.

"Hell yeah. I was just telling Dallas and Neysa in our group message that I needed to get out and have some fun. Traveling and working all the time…. I be too tired to see what other states have to offer by the time I'm done working." Shonnie explained, pulling up in front of the club.

"Don't I know the feeling… Aye, you think Dallas and Neysa gon' be cool with me crashing y'all outing? I know how bitches can get when they friend bring a friend." Trinity semi-joked, knowing how petty women could actually be.

"Bitch, stop. You know I don't fuck with dem type of bitches. I mean, Dallas and Neysa ain't changed much since high school and y'all was cool back then."

"No. Y'ALL was cool back then. I just know them in passing; however, I'm friends with Neysa on Facebook and she seem cool. I heard Dallas owns her own tattoo shop or sum like that…." Trinity recalled, finally stepping out of the car.

"Yup! It's called Queenz Tatt. It's an all-female staffed tattoo shop downtown. Dallas be hiring some of the dopiest artist from around the world. Paying dem hoes big bucks to come work for her…. I'm the bitch friend, and I can't even get an appointment." Shonnie laughed, causing Trinity to chuckle too.

Hearing the way Shonnie spoke about her other friends made her feel much more comfortable. Trinity was in no way shape, form, or fashion intimated by either of them; she just wanted to ensure that she was surrounded by positive vibes.

"Look, Boogie at the door. Come on." Shonnie pointed out, locking arms with Trinity as they walked past everyone in line.

Hearing the loud smacks and rude comments from the hating women in the line only made Trinity toss her braids to the back and put a little more switch in her walk. She was loving the moment, and although there was nothing like Atlanta's night life, no other city compared to summertime in the Chi.

Just like she expected, Trell's party was packed with people and full of energy. Half-naked bottle girls walked in a line, floating sparkling bottles of Ace of Spades above everyone's head. The DJ played the latest hits while the dance floor was filled to capacity. The club was sectioned off with a few VIP areas and a huge stage sat far back in the cut.

"I wonder if they gon' have a performance." Shonnie leaned over and yelled inside Trinity's ear over the loud music.

"You must have been reading my mind girl." Trinity laughed as they held hands, maneuvering through the crowd towards the bar.

"Let's get a drink. As a matter of fact, I know Trell got hella drinks in his section…. Let's head over there first." Shonnie directed, pulling Trinity towards one of the crowded VIP sections.

Attempting to pull her dress down and walk without bumping into people, Trinity struggled across the club while Shonnie led the way like a supermodel on the runway. Finally reaching their section, Trinity tugged at her dress one last time before standing up straight, adjusting and focusing her eyes on the things in front of her.

"DAMN!" She grimaced louder than she thought, causing Shonnie to shoot her a look.

Purposely ignoring her stares, Trinity looked around at any and everything except her friend.

"Nah, Nah, Nah…. I know what that *DAMN* mean. Who you looking at Trini?" Shonnie questioned, still having the ability to read her like a book.

Trinity laughed as her friend's eyes searched the section, trying to guess who had her attention. She laughed even harder when Shonnie began tossing out names as a final desperate attempt.

"Who you looking at bitch? Tony? The one in the red? Or the one with the hat… ugh friend, he ugly. I know you ain't thinking about Vonte bean head ass or Trell…. You know Ocean and Chinks from school…. Those about the only ones worth looking at, sooooooo…. which one?"

Shonnie rambled on and on as Trinity bent over in laughter, almost forgetting that her ass was already half out. Shonnie was so nosey, never took no for an answer, and on top of all that, she thought she was cupid. Always trying to match people up.

"Let's go girl." Trinity said, finally gaining her composure, pulling Shonnie along, leading the way this time.

Stepping behind the rope, Trinity felt like all eyes were on her. True enough, half of the section was filled with classmates from high school, and she had been off the radar for a few years, but they were acting as if they saw Casper, the friendly ghost.

"Damn, what up Trinity." A few whispered as she passed by, grabbing her hand while she wisped past them.

Speaking and keeping it moving, she followed behind Shonnie until she reached the plush black and gold couch, where most of the women were seated.

"Hey y'all. Y'all remember Trinity from high school? Trinity, this is Neysa and Dallas." Shonnie announced, warmly introducing the group of women.

All four women stood around smiling, dishing out hugs like they were in church instead of the club. Both women seemed welcoming, making Trinity feel much more comfortable.

"WHAT Y'ALL DRINKING?" A thick Latina waitress asked as the girls shouted out their orders.

Placing her drink order along with the others, Trinity sat down next to Shonnie, where she began to vibe with the music. Everything was going great; there was no negative energy, and niggas was acting civilized; this was definitely Trinity's speed.

CHAPTER FOUR

The liquor was flowing, the music was blasting, and everyone was having a good time. Dallas was beyond happy that her girls agreed to hang with her. She usually had an attitude when they brought a plus one along, but Trinity seemed cool and Shonnie always spoke fond of her.

Dallas's eyes searched the crowd, stopping on her husband who rapped along to Young Jeezy's first album, completely in his own zone. The gold Rolex glistened on his wrist while he held a cup of dark liquor in the other hand. Marquis "Chinks" Moore had the same effect on Dallas all these years later, having the ability to make her pussy throb just by standing there, doing nothing. She loved her husband with every fiber bone in her body; he was truly her partner in crime, and if things went as planned, they'll have another victim by the end of the night.

"You sitting over here staring at a nigga like you wanna fuck." Chinks walked up and stated, completely catching her off guard.

She had been so thrown off daydreaming about him, she hadn't even noticed him heading her way. Looking him up and down in the all black he wore, Dallas felt her pussy tingling again. She wasn't sure if it was liquor or the fact she hadn't had dick in seven days, but whichever one it was, had her feeling like a nympho.

Standing to her feet in the black and silver six-inch Balenciaga heels, Dallas adjusted the Fendi crop top she wore before stepping in close to Chinks. His deep beady eyes stared into hers, the Henny on his breath caused goosebumps to form on the back of her neck.

"I'll fuck the shit outta you right now but...... I got better plans for us later." Dallas leaned in and seductively spoke before moving and standing on the side of him.

"Straight ahead.... Shorty in the red dress." She paused before gliding back in front of him.

"I want my pussy ate tonight.... Double tongues though." She winked at him as a grin slowly appeared on his face.

Dallas spotted Shanae the moment she walked through the door; her pussy instantly began to throb as she thought back to the last encounter they had. Meeting her a few months back at the shop, Shanae came in for a tattoo but left with much more. Being friends with her head tattoo artist, Shannon, Shanae started hanging around often, eventually becoming a "friend" to Dallas as well.

"Set it up. I ain't trying to be here long anyway." Chinks finally replied, pulling out his phone, checking the time on the screen.

Nodding her head up and down in agreement, Dallas walked away, heading back over to the couch to summon her girls.

"I'm going to the bathroom." She whispered loudly over the music, leaning in close to both Neysa and Shonnie.

"We gon' come with you. Come on Trinity." Shonnie stood to her feet and replied, tugging at Trinity so that she could join them as well.

Walking hand by hand, forming a line, the four women made their way through the crowded VIP section as well as the busy dance floor to the restroom located on the opposite side of the club. After speaking to a few familiar faces as she passed by, Dallas and her crew stood at the door, in line again, behind two other women.

"Trinity, how have you been? I haven't seen you since high school. You look great." Dallas turned to her and complicated, looking her over a final time.

"Thanks, girl. You been a bad bitch since high school, but I'm good. Just moved back in town… trying to adjust." She smiled, showing off a perfect set of teeth and deep dimples to match.

Moving along in the line, Dallas entered the bathroom with her girls behind her, heading straight to the full-length mirror that was in the back. Twirling and twisting from side to side, Dallas made sure everything was intact before leaving back out. Snatching a sheet of paper towel from the dispenser, she used it to open the door, disappearing in the crowd.

"I'll meet y'all back at the section. I'm going to the bar." Dallas yelled to Neysa just as the beat dropped to Lil Baby's latest hit.

Neysa shot Dallas a look that made her smile; they had been friends since they were ten, and if anyone knew her, it was definitely Neysa Brown. Gliding through the dance floor, Dallas head bobbed to the beat as she made it to her destination. Just as she slid up to the bar, Shanae turned around and greeted her with a smile.

"Long time no see." She huffed, playfully rolling her eyes to the back of her head.

"So, I see. How you been?" Dallas asked with a smile, truthfully not caring but in need of small talk.

"I been good. No complaints. What about you Mrs. Moore? You still fine as fuck." Shanae complimented, looking Dallas up and down from head to toe.

Noticing the flirtatious look in Shanae's eyes, Dallas used that as an opportunity to wheel her in. Stepping in close to her, Dallas invaded her personal space, so close that their breasts touched. Dallas's eyes traveled from Shanae's perky double D's to her face before back down to her breasts.

"You coming home with me tonight?" Dallas asked, circling Shanae's nipples with the tip of her long nails.

Without verbal clarification, Shanae placed her drink on the counter, picked up her clutch, and locked arms with Dallas. Tickled by her enthusiasm, Dallas headed back over to the VIP section with her "new friend" in tow. Locking eyes with Chinks who gave a slight grin, Dallas winked her eye at him before taking a seat.

"Aye best friend. I'm about to head out. I'll see you in the morning." Dallas leaned over and announced, placing a kiss on Neysa's cheek.

"Shonnie. I'll see you later. Trinity, it was nice seeing you again." Dallas continued with her goodbyes before officially parting ways.

Slipping out the way she came in, she held hands with Shanae as they made their way out of the club and to her white Range Rover. Hearing the alarm beep, Dallas turned around and smirked before focusing her attention ahead.

"Heyyyy Chinks!" Shanae seductively spoke, noticing him approaching as well.

"What up shorty?" He greeted her with a head nod before hopping in the driver's seat of his wife's ride.

Reaching for the door handle on her Range Rover, Dallas was stopped by Shanae, and from the look in her eyes, she knew why.

"I don't wanna wait to taste it." Shanae specified, causing the biggest smile to form on Dallas's horny face.

Without thinking twice, Dallas headed to the back seat with Shanae while Chinks acted as their chauffeur. Wasting no time, Shanae pulled Dallas close to her, their tongues engaged in an intense game of *Twister*. Imagining the damage that tongue could do to her pussy, Dallas lifted up the Chanel skirt she was wearing while Shanae pushed her back onto the leather seats. Within a matter of seconds, Shanae was placing soft kisses in between her thighs, forcing her to close her eyes.

Briefly opening her eyes, Dallas noticed Chinks looking at them out of the rearview mirror. Ready to enjoy to what she had to offer, Dallas pushed Shanae's head down deep in between her legs, where she began to explore. Ravishing in the moment, Dallas rode Shanae's tongue while Chinks did seventy miles per hour on the expressway. The fast speed mixed with the marvelous head had her adrenaline rushing, causing her to cum prematurely.

The one thing the couple loved most about Shanae was that she was an eater, meaning, once she got started, there was no stopping her. Pinning Dallas's legs further back, Shanae dove back in, cleaning up the mess she caused, only to make a bigger mess.

"Y'all wanna take this inside?" Dallas heard Chinks say, just as the car was thrown into park.

"No--- No---No. Come back here with us." She requested through loud moans as he followed her instructions, fulfilling their night and threesome in the back of her ride.

CHAPTER FIVE

Neysa snatched up her car keys and ran down the basement stairs to meet Ocean, who was waiting for her there. Turning the corner, an instant attitude came over her as she watched her man snoring loudly with his head titled back.

"Ocean. Wake up!" she nudged at him, causing him to stir in his sleep.

"WAKE UP!" She yelled, this time getting the reaction that she wanted.

"Damn man, I'm high as fuck. What time is it?" he asked, looking around trying to find his phone or the remote control.

"It's almost three and the party started an hour ago. Ocean get uppppp!" she whined, tugging at his huge body, not moving him an inch.

"Aight baby. Let's go." He finally replied, standing to his feet, adjusting his clothes, leading the way out the door.

Neysa smiled to herself, completely shocked by Ocean's response; however, she went with the flow. He hated anything involving her parents, which is why she was surprised that he agreed to go over there. Neysa's nephew,

Eric, birthday was today, and they were celebrating by having cake and ice cream at her parents' house.

"An hour Neysa and then we out. You know I don't fuck with yo people like that." Ocean grimaced as they headed to his Jeep.

Not wanting to expand on the conversation, Neysa remained quiet the entire ride to her parents' house. Ocean and his dislike for her family was no secret; however, Neysa was tired of hearing the shit.

"Good. It looks like everybody here already." She sighed, noticing the familiar cars parked along the residential street.

The deep breath from Ocean indicated that he was ready to go already, and they had yet exited the vehicle. Unbuckling her seatbelt, Neysa stepped out in her YSL sandals and long flowy maxi dress from Fashion Nova. It was another hot day in Chicago, but Neysa loved each and every moment of it.

"Bae, don't forget Eric's gift in the back." She reminded him as she headed across the lawn to the backyard.

Stopping once out of the grass, Neysa waited for Ocean, who walked towards her with a shiny blue Fortnite gift bag in hand.

"Damn you look beautiful." He drooled, stepping in, placing kisses on her neck.

Neysa blushed and squirmed as his full lips touched her soft brown skin. She wanted to say, *fuck them kids*, and head back home, but it was too late; they were already spotted.

"Ewwwww.... this is a kid's party." Nicole, her sister, scolded as she headed out the house with a pan of ribs.

"Shut up bitch." Neysa cursed, smiling at the disgusted look on her fat face.

"Ummmm Ocean.... here negro." She snapped, shoving out the pan of ribs in his direction.

Neysa laughed before looking over at Ocean, who shook his head from side to side. Nicole was controlling, and she didn't give a fuck about who you were.

"Anything for my favorite sister-in-law." He chuckled, grabbing the dish and walking off.

"I'M YO ONLY SISTER IN-LAW NIGGA!" she yelled out before the two embraced each other with a hug.

"Ooooohhh Weeee! You look good sis!" Neysa exclaimed, spinning Nicole around as if they were dancing.

"Keto, bitch. Keto." She sang before doing the most awful twerk Neysa had ever seen in her life.

Nicole was Korean and Black, Neysa's half-sister, but you couldn't dare tell them that. They'll swear on a Bible that the same blood flowed through their veins. They were thicker than thieves, and it had been that way since they met at six-years-old.

"Where Mommy and Appa *(Dad in Korean)?"* Neysa quizzed, looking around Nicole and into the backyard.

"They back there…. As a matter of fact…." Nicole paused, turning around, looking back herself.

"We may need to get back there before Ocean shoot the whole backyard up." Nicole laughed, bending over, holding her stomach at her own joke.

"GIRL, FUCK YOU!" Neysa cursed, pushing her out the way to check on her man.

Neysa and Ocean's relationship was the talk of the family, even after being together for ten years. Her family, mostly her parents, despised Ocean and disapproved highly of their relationship.

Neysa Brown, daughter to Pam and Lee Sui; scholar, trained ballet dancer, fluent in three languages, and mathematician. There was no way in the world she belonged with a hood nigga. A man with no high school diploma or GED. A street pharmacist, a pistol totting, future Kingpin.

"Hey everybody!" Neysa greeted the many guests that occupied her parents' enormous backyard.

Everyone sang their hellos just as Eric came crashing at her knees. Smiling, looking down at her favorite kid in the world, Neysa scooped up her nephew before spinning him around.

"How old are you today, TT Big Man?" she excitedly asked, slowly placing him back on his feet.

"I'm three Auntie!" his little voice yelled over the Kid's Bop that played loudly on the speakers.

Surveilling her surroundings, Neysa spotted Ocean off in the corner in a lounge chair, buried in his phone.

"You hungry? Want something to drink?" she walked over to him and asked, flopping down on his lap.

"Nah, I'm straight. Go grab Eric for me, so I can give him his gift." Ocean requested, smacking Neysa on the ass as she headed over to her nephew.

After sending him Ocean's way, she went inside the house to get a break from the heat and to use the bathroom. Slipping into the basement unnoticed, Neysa used the toilet down there before returning back out.

"There she go right there. Neysa, come here."

Rolling her eyes to the back of her head, Neysa put on a fake smile before turning around, greeting her mom. The sound of her voice made her skin crawl, specifically the way she called her name.

"I didn't know you was here yet. I was just about to call you and tell you to grab some candles on your way over." Pam stated as Neysa climbed the steps, entering the kitchen.

"It's cool. I'll have Ocean run down to Walgreens and…"

"NAH! That's ok. I don't need HIM doing shit for me, as a matter of fact…."

"Bye mom." Neysa cut her off, raising her hand high in the air, turning to leave when her dad stopped her.

"Neysa, come back." He spoke, his broken English improved so much over the years.

"No baby, let her go. She hates to hear the truth when it comes to *that* man." Pam spoke calmly, stirring the spaghetti that was on the stove.

"Since when has your opinion become the truth?" Neysa's neck snapped in the direction of her mom and questioned.

"Come on y'all.... DAMN! It's my son's party. Can we get along for once?" Nicole appeared from the back and cursed, causing all eyes to dart in her direction.

When it came to the never-ending battle regarding her relationship, Nicole was the only person who had Neysa's back. Over the years, she had her moments when she too hated Ocean; however, that was based off the things he had done, unlike with her parents.

"All those years of training and education gone down the drain. All our hard work." Pam cried out hysterically, making a scene like she always did.

"She's so fuckn' dramatic. I'm gone." Neysa laughed before chucking up the deuces and walking away.

She had heard enough, and if she stayed any longer, she was liable to hurt some feelings. It never failed, each and every time Ocean's name was mentioned in the presence of Pam, she always had something negative to say. It was one thing disliking a person but being disrespectful was not tolerated, regardless of who you were.

"Listen to her. Cursing and carrying on. I bet she gets that hood shit from him." Neysa heard her mom yell out from the top of the stairs.

"NO! NO! NO! PAM. I GET THAT HOOD SHIT FROM ***YOU*** OR DID YOU FORGET YOU WERE A PRODUCT OF THE HOOD YOURSELF?"

"Neysa, sis, let's go outside." Nicole tried intervening, but it was too late.

"Or ma, did you forget that my FATHER, may he rest in peace, was one of those "thugs" you refer to Ocean as?" Neysa yanked away from Nicole who was now tugging at her elbow.

"NEYSA SUI…" her stepdad yelled out, his finger pointing directly in her face.

"MY LAST NAME IS ***BROWN***!" she yelled back, stepping forward, challenging everyone in the room.

Silence fell amongst everyone, who looked around at each other's face. Neysa refused to back down, and truthfully, she was tired of their shit. Just as she fixed her mouth to give them another piece of her mind, footsteps were heard from behind her, but when she turned around, it was already too late.

"Why the fu- Why his finger in yo face?" Ocean appeared out of nowhere and asked, ready to body Neysa's dad right there in his own kitchen.

"I'm good, baby. Let's go." She turned to him and said calmly, pushing him in his chest, trying to deescalate the situation.

It was one thing getting her started, but once Ocean got involved, all hell could break loose.

CHAPTER SIX

"Come innnnnn." Trinity's soft voice sang from behind her MacBook Pro to the visitor at the other end of her office door.

Standing to her feet, Trinity smoothed out the wrinkles in her maroon pencil skirt before closing her laptop shut. Noticing that it was noon, thoughts of lunch plagued her mind and empty stomach as she thought about what she should eat. Chipotle, her favorite, popped in her head first, and she decided to go with a steak bowl from there.

"Damn shame I gotta make an appointment to see my own baby."

The biggest smile ever invaded her face as she heard her Aunt Shelia's raspy voice. Lifting her head slowly, Trinity closed the Chipotle app before eagerly making her way around the cherry oakwood desk and into her aunt's arms. Feeling like a baby, Trinity wanted to cry like one; she was happy and seeing her favorite aunt was exactly what she needed.

"What you doing down here?" Trinity asked, releasing from their embrace and taking a seat on the edge of her desk.

"Well.... I was shopping down here and decided to stop by seeing how that's the only way Imma ever see you." She replied, flopping down in the black lounge chair near her.

"Honestly Auntie, I was coming by to see you today. I've been so busy and...."

"Yeah. Yeah. Yeah. I hear you Trini. I hear you." Shelia waved her off, causing Trinity to laugh.

"I'm for real TeeTee. Listen." She begged, standing to her feet to answer her office phone.

After canceling her remaining meetings for the day, Trinity grabbed her laptop and everything she needed to work from home and locked up her office. Nothing was more important than spending time with the woman who raised her and that's what she intended on doing. Sliding to a nice black owned coffee shop up the street, Trinity ordered a cup of coffee and bagel to curve her appetite a little. She had every intention on getting her Chipotle, even if that meant waiting until dinner.

"So, Auntie, what's been going on with you. You look gorgeous." Trinity complimented, taking a sip from the Columbian brew in her cup.

"Traveling. Enjoying life. You know y'all kids...."

"Slowed you down. You were supposed to be married to LL Cool J by now… Auntie, I know the story." Trinity giggled, cutting her off in mid-sentence, finishing the thought for her.

Auntie Shelia loved and raised Trinity as if she was the one who birthed her. Nancy, her biological mother, died from complications with pneumonia; however, Trinity later learned her mother passed away from AIDS. At twelve-years old, she moved from Atlanta to Chicago, where Aunt Shelia stepped in and took over for her baby sister. Caring for Trinity along with her only son, Roy, Shelia did the best she could, ultimately being the best thing that ever happened to Trini.

"How's Roy? You talk to him?" Trinity asked from across the table as her aunties' eyes wondered around the coffee shop.

"Nope. His ass still in the hole. I just don't understand that jail shit, but then again, it ain't meant for me to get it. It's a place I'll never be."

Roy was serving a life sentence for murdering his ex-girlfriend and unborn child ten years ago. Trying to be the best mother possible, Shelia stayed by his side the best she could over the years, but from the look on her face, that time was coming to an end.

"I'll check on some things when I get back to work, maybe he…."

"Let him be, Trinity. You got better things to worry about like, scheduling you a date to take the bar exam…."

And just like that, Aunt Shelia sounded like Charlie Brown's teacher, Ms. Othmar. Her words were like a foreign language, going in one ear and out the other. Trinity knew it was only a matter of time before the "lawyer conversation" were brought into play, and just like the many times before, she wasn't trying to hear it.

" TeeTee, I'm young, I still have time to be a lawyer. You sound like Shonnie." She replied, thinking back to the last talk she had with her friend regarding the same topic.

"Ohhhh Shonnie. How has she been? What about Gloria? She's good?" Aunt Shelia questioned before breaking off a piece of bagel and stuffing it in her mouth.

Trinity filled her aunt in while they ordered more coffee and sweet treats. It felt so good catching up with her versus doing so over the phone, and Trinity missed her more than anybody else. Her Aunt Shelia was her rock, the reason she was the successful woman she was at the tender age of twenty-six. Trinity planned on paying her aunt back, even if that meant becoming that infamous lawyer she always wanted her to be.

"Speaking of men. When you gon' get one?"

"Auntie, wasn't nobody talking about men. I was telling you how Shonnie has a gig with VH1 on the set of one of their shows. What are you talking about?" Trinity laughed at her aunt's nosey ways.

The word "man" hadn't been bought up, but Aunt Shelia found a way to pry inside of Trinity's love life.

"Chillleeeee… I thought you said something about a man, my bad but since we on the subject now. When you gon' get one?"

Bursting out in laughter, Trinity drew a couple of eyes, but she could care less; she was a firm believer that people should mind the business that pays them.

"I'm single TeeTee, and I'm perfectly fine with that. You know I was seeing someone before I moved back; however, we decided to break things off."

"Why?" she leaned in forward and pondered.

"Because of the distance, Auntie. It'll never work out. I rather work on rebuilding here first and worry about a man later. Is that okay with you?"

Trinity's aunt's eyes grew the size of golf balls with every word she spoke. She knew Shelia didn't like the answers she was receiving, but she'll be okay, especially since the real truth would break her fragile heart.

"You better watch yo mouth. I paid for them braces, and I'll pay for some more." Aunt Shelia snapped, the loose salt and pepper curls shaking in her head.

"What Auntie?" Trinity twisted her neck to the side and asked with a confused smirk on her face.

"You talk to me crazy again, you gon' need a new grill.... You understand now?" Shelia responded sharply, putting Trinity in her place.

Taking another sip from her coffee, Trinity decided to remain quiet, not only because Aunt Shelia was good for her word, but also because, Trinity didn't have the guts to tell her what was really going on in her love life.

CHAPTER SEVEN

Dallas looked over the detailed black and gold rose on her client's back and smiled. It wasn't often she did tattoos herself, she preferred for her ladies to eat; therefore, she only did special request, usually for family, close friends, and millionaires. Admiring her own work, Dallas felt a sense of pride mixed with cockiness as she wiped away the excess ink.

"Zone, you all set!" she announced, standing to her feet and walking over to the full-length mirror that hung in the booth.

Handing Chicago's hottest rapper, Zone, the pink glittery hand mirror to check his reflection, Dallas stood back and blushed at his reaction.

"This shit so fuckn' dope G, good looking baby." He boosted, checking himself out at all angles, twisting and turning, trying to get the best view.

"I mean.... I do a little something." She modestly bragged, glancing down at the ringing phone on the tray.

"Zarkia got all yo after care products up front. She'll give them to you once you check out. We can do a coloring session in three weeks once the peeling is done. I wanna go over the petals one more time."

Wrapping things up with Zone, Dallas cleaned the booth before retreating to her office to grab her gym bag. She was meeting Neysa and Shonnie for their weekly workout at Planet Fitness, up the street from her shop. It had been a long weekend and considering how many carbs alcohol contained, she needed to be on someone's treadmill quick, fast and in a hurry.

"Fuck!" she cursed under her breath just as there was a knock on the door.

It never failed; it seemed as if every time she tried to dip away to do something for herself, she was always pulled into something else, something definitely less interesting. Strutting over in her blue and white Air Max 95s, Dallas pulled the door back without asking who was on the other end. Immediately bursting out in laughter at the look on her mother's face, Dallas stood there, trying to be serious.

"Ma. I told you that I was going to bring the keys to you. Why you drive all the way down here?" Dallas asked Oliva, who pushed her way passed her daughter and into her office.

"Well Justine drove, and I needed to get out the house anyway. We gon' stop and grab a corn beef sandwich from Manny's since we in the neighborhood." She responded from her spot in the middle of the floor.

"Looks like you were heading out. Where you going?" her mother continued, shifting her Gucci bag from one shoulder to the other.

"To the gym. Why mommy ain't come in and see me?" Dallas asked with an angry face, folding her arms across her chest.

"She's double parked. I was supposed to be running in and back out."

It had been a week since Dallas last seen her parents. They took a cruise to the Bahamas to celebrate their anniversary. Married in 2014 after legalizing gay marriages, Oliva and Justine meet forty years prior to that. Adopting a precious baby girl, who was left at a local fire station in 1997, changed the couple's life forever.

"Ok well here. I'll be over later today still to talk to y'all." Dallas advised, handing her the keys to the car and walking towards the door.

She was already running late and knowing her friends, they were cursing her out about it at that very moment. Hugging her mom goodbye, Dallas locked up before splitting ways with her, leaving out the back door.

Wasting no time, Dallas sped the entire way down Roosevelt to her destination, arriving seven minutes later. Jumping out, Dallas noticed Shonnie's car parked a few spaces over and shook her head. She was the most anal when it came to time management, so Dallas knew she was definitely going to hear her mouth.

"If my mother wouldn't have stopped by the shop, I would have been on time." She walked in the locker room and stated the moment she seen Shonnie's face.

"Un huh. You lucky cuz if I hadn't picked up Trinity, I would have been waiting nine hours on you." She exaggerated as she adjusted the red and black Ka'Oir waist trainer around her waist.

Instead of responding, Dallas got dressed in her workout gear before filling her water bottle up to the top. After snatching a towel out of her gym bag, she joined Shonnie on the floor near the treadmills.

"Trinity, hey girl." Dallas greeted her with a warm smile before starting the machine next to her.

Securing the air pods in her ear, Dallas tuned into Trey Songz station on the Pandora app, selected incline on the machine, and started her workout. An hour later and a few calories less, Dallas was roasting in the sauna with her girls, gossiping.

"What happened to Neysa? I thought y'all said she was coming too." Trinity asked, taking a seat directly across from Dallas.

"I still haven't talked to her. Maybe she got called in." Shonnie replied from her spot on the bench.

"Nah, she's on vacation. Let me text her now." Dallas stated, picking up her phone and dialing her best friend's number.

After getting no answer, she shot her a text, just to make sure that everything was alright. It was not like Neysa to be late or especially do a no call no show.

"So, I haven't seen you ladies since the club. What's been up?" Trinity stated with a warm smile, a smile that Dallas hadn't noticed before.

This was only Dallas's second time seeing the girl since high school, and she knew little to nothing about her. Of course, Shonnie bragged about Trinity like she did all her friends, but the two ladies never had an one on one.

"Girl, that night, I stopped at White Castles and took my ass home. What about y'all? You dipped out early

Dallas, what's up?" Shonnie turned to her and asked, a mischievous grin planted on her pudgy face.

"Wait. Did I miss something?" Trinity questioned, her eyes shifting back and forth between Shonnie and Dallas.

"Welllll…. Since yo nosey ass asking…. We went home early and…"

"Who is WE?" Shonnie cut her off and asked, knowing Dallas far too well.

Smiling from ear to ear, Dallas shook her head from side to side as both women watched her closely. She knew there was no sense in lying to Shonnie and Trinity didn't know her, so her opinion didn't matter.

"Remember Shanae from…."

"You fuckn' on that girl again, Dallas?" Shonnie blurted out, interrupting her for the second time that day.

Shamefully, Dallas buried her face inside the palm of her hands and chuckled lightly.

"I know. I know. I know. But I swear that was the *last* time." She lifted her head and admitted truthfully.

Dallas and Chinks had outgrown Shanae and their last sexual encounter proved that. After the night of the party, Shanae went back to her crazy ways. Blowing both of their phones up and popping up unannounced at both of their places of business. Because she always kept it respectful, Dallas never had to go upside her head, but she felt her patience running thin.

"She been popping up at my job as well as Chinks's Auto Shop. I don't know what's wrong with the girl, but she got one more time and Imma have Shay Shay and nem stomp her face in."

Dallas planned on keeping her word if Shanae got out of pocket again. Her favorite little cousin Shay Shay and her homegirls beat bitches for a living, and they'll do the job for free if Dallas asked.

"Aye, remember that time Shay Shay and Nikki chased Kinisha down 16th street that summer?" Shonnie recalled, bending over, holding her stomach laughing.

Rolling her eyes to the back of her head, Dallas thought back on that event and all the others involving her husband's ex, Kinisha. Minus the incident recently, she had been M.I.A and that's the way Dallas liked it.

"Wait. What Kinisha? Kinisha Harry from high school?" Trinity quizzed with beady eyes as if she was trying to crack the case.

"Girl, yeah. You know her and Chinks dated while him and Dallas took a break. Kinisha used to be soooo thirsty for him…"

"And she still is." Dallas cut Shonnie off and stated, flipping her long hair over her shoulders.

It was true, out of their five years of marriage, Chinks had been unfaithful once, or at least been caught. Admitting having caught feelings for Kinisha while during a break, Chinks swore on his life that he would never dip back into that pot again.

"But back to you and yo sexual fantasies…."

"Ain't no fantasies. Me and my husband love fucking bitches together, time to time. You and Neysa act like it's an everyday routine of ours. The shit happens once every blue moon." Dallas defended, catching a slight attitude in the process.

Dallas and Chinks didn't have an open relationship like many thought they did. Both of them were faithful, but the both of them were freaks. Bringing victims inside the bedroom was something they did maybe four times a year, and Shanae was the last. It's not like they went on the pry looking for threesomes; they just so happen to fall in their laps.

"Time out. This seems interesting. Tell me more." Trinity interrupted with a joke, standing up and taking a seat next to Dallas now.

"NO! NO! Don't you start. It's bad enough I gotta hear it from Dallas. Trinity, not you too." Shonnie grimaced, dapping her forehead with her towel.

"Wait! What she mean don't get you started? What you been doing in Atlanta?" Dallas turned to Trinity and asked, eyeing her suspiciously.

Trinity's hazel eyes danced around the sauna before she buried her face inside the palm of her hands. Dallas knew that body language far too well. Ms. Trinity had a few skeletons in her closet.

"Okay! Hold up you freaks. We not finna have this conversation right here." Shonnie raised her hands in the air and contested.

"And why not?" Dallas snapped her head in her direction and questioned, playfully rolling her eyes.

"Yeah Shonnie. Why can't grown women have grown women conversations?" Trinity followed behind her and quizzed.

Trinity was seemingly coming out of her shell, and Dallas was enjoying it. Unsure if it was the steam from the sauna or the hot topic they were having, but Dallas was feeling horny. Grabbing her phone, she ignored the awaiting text from Neysa and messaged Chinks instead. She needed him to meet her at home ASAP. His dick was calling her name.

CHAPTER EIGHT

Neysa placed her overnight Louie Vuitton mini-duffle bag on the counter and picked up the mail sitting next to it. Smiling at the name on the envelope, Neysa ripped it open and read over the contents aloud.

"You are cordially invited to Maggie's Twelve-Year-Old Pool Bash…."

After reading the remaining details, such as the date and time, Neysa took the postcard and placed it on the refrigerator, using a magnet. She loved Maggie and wouldn't miss her party for nothing in the world.

TWO YEARS AGO

"Hey sweetheart, how are you? I'm Dr. Brown. I heard you were in a car accident today and was hurt pretty badly. Can you show me where it hurts?"

Neysa took a few steps back and watched as the fragile ten-year-old struggled to keep her eyes open. Stepping forward and even closer than before, Neysa used her hands to aid as back support for the child.

"It's okay, baby. Let's try something else. I'm going to press softly on your stomach. Let me know if it hurts, okay?"

Doing as she promised, Neysa used her left hand to press very lightly on her stomach.

"Ouch!" she jumped while Neysa rubbed her back softly in circles.

"Ok Maggie, lay back for me. I'll be back in a second." Neysa assured with a warm smile, pulling the thin hospital sheets up to her neck.

"Mommy and Daddy, can I speak with you for a second? We'll be right back sweetheart." Neysa promised her small patient again before leaving out the room.

Once inside the hallway, she waited until the door was closed before addressing the older black couple. Taking a deep breath, Neysa noticed the worried look on their faces and could only imagine how scared they were.

"Maggie's an amazing kid." She paused, looking back at the room door before focusing her attention to Mr. and Mrs. Miller.

"Dr. Bose is Maggie's Physician and as you know, I was simply stopping by checking on her. I see in Maggie's charts that she had an X-Ray done when she came in earlier, however...."

"Mr. and Mrs. Miller, I'm Dr. Bose, Maggie's Physician." She walked up, interrupting Neysa and introducing herself.

Dr. Bose cut her eyes at Neysa before continuing, "Did you have any questions for me? Resident Brown...."

"DOCTOR BROWN!" Neysa cut her off and checked, catching all the shade being thrown her way.

Dr. Bose had been a pain in Neysa's ass since the day she was assigned to that floor. An older white lady in her late fifties couldn't stand to see a young black doctor with better credentials than her, stepping in and outshining her. Therefore, whenever her and Neysa crossed paths, she made it a living hell.

"Well as a matter of fact, Dr. Brown here was speaking to us about Maggie's charts, and we'll like to hear more about that." Mrs. Miller stepped in and explained as her husband shook his head up and down in agreement.

"Well as I was saying, the initial test shows that everything is fine; however, I think we should send her back for an X-Ray, ASAP!" Neysa urged as the eyes on all three people in front of her widen.

"NO. There's no need for a second one. The results we have is fine, I've been a doctor longer than you've been born and...."

"And I can give two shits about any of that. Maggie is showing signs of internal bleeding. If we don't get a second X-Ray as soon as possible, it may be too late."

Silence fell upon the small area next to the room as everyone searched for their own rebuttal. It was true, Dr. Bose had been practicing longer and was probably more knowledgeable, but Neysa knew what she was talking about and would bet her last dime on it.

"Mr. and Mrs. Miller, I suggest you request a second X-Ray. Tell Maggie I'll be by to check on her later. You two take care." Neysa turned to the parents and stated with a sincere smile.

Present Day

After saving Maggie's life, the Millers made sure they kept in touch, even making Neysa and Ocean, Maggie's honorary God Parents. The love Neysa had for that little girl was like no other, and she vowed to always be in her life.

Making sure to set the alarm, Neysa headed to her car, tossing her overnight bag in the backseat before taking off. Stopping at Binny's up the street, Neysa grabbed two pints of Patron and four bottles of Stella Rosa wine. Finally headed to Shonnie's place now, she connected her phone, allowing Summer Walker's voice to lead the way.

Twenty minutes later, Neysa was finding a parking spot not far from Shonnie's condo. Since flaking on the girls last week at the gym, Neysa knew she couldn't miss their lady's night sleepover. Shonnie was leaving for Utah in the morning and then going on the road for two months straight, doing makeup for the stars. This was the last time she would see her friend for a while and planned on making it a night to remember.

After being buzzed in, Neysa took the elevator to the sixth floor where she took the long hall down to Shonnie's front door. Knocking twice, Neysa could hear music playing from the other side of the door. Swaying her hips from side to side with the beat, Neysa enjoyed the old music moments before the door swung open.

"I told you not to bring nothing. I already had everything here." Shonnie fussed, snatching the bags of liquor from her hands and disappearing in the house.

Closing the door behind her, Neysa laughed as Dallas and Trinity held a dance contest in the middle of the floor. Admiring both of their moves, Neysa made her way inside the kitchen to help Shonnie unload the bags.

"Girl, you trying to get us fucked up, huh?" Shonnie asked, holding both bottles of Patron high in the air.

"Trinity got Don Julio and Dallas brought Hennessey. You bitches gon' make me miss my flight." She continued, pulling Neysa a wine glass from the cabinet.

"Well it looks like y'all got the party started without me. Them two hoes in there already loose." she replied, using the corkscrew to loosen up the bottle.

"Well, you know how Dallas is and Trinity.... Well...."

"Dallas and Trinity what?"

"Yeah, y'all in here talking shit about us?" Trinity followed behind Dallas and added in, leaning against the bar.

Both Neysa and Trinity bussed out in laughter while the other two ladies looked around and wondered what the joke was. It was Neysa's second time kicking it with Trinity, and although it took a lot for her to like new people, she welcomed her with open arms.

"A toast. A toast to my friend's new journey." Dallas grabbed a shot glass full of clear liquor and raised it high.

"Right D. A toast to being a bad bitch at beating these bitches' faces." Neysa followed behind her and announced, doing the same with her glass.

"I'm so proud of you, and although you are leaving me alone for months, I couldn't be happier for you friend." Trinity ended the speech with as all four ladies' glasses collided before they tossed back the hard liquor.

"I love y'all so much. Thanks for always being there for me and supporting me through it all. Trini, I'll be back before you know it." Shonnie promised, using her hands to fan her eyes as tears threated her perfect makeup.

"Aye. Aye. Aye. Stop with all that mushy shit. It's only two months." Dallas playfully stated, lightening the mood in the kitchen.

"Right. We gon' look after Trinity while you gone and when you get back……BITCH THE MARTHON CONTINUES!" Neysa shouted loudly before pouring another round of shots.

After the third round of Patron, the ladies were ready to get their night started. Neysa and Dallas showered in each of Shonnie's bathrooms while her and Trinity ordered the food. Once Neysa and Dallas was done, they switched roles; however, they made drinks and found a movie to watch instead.

Each dressed in Calvin Klein's tanks and shorts, grabbed their wine glasses, and found a comfy spot on the plush couch. Ten minutes into "Waiting to Exhale," UberEats came arriving with their pizza, wings, and desserts. Acting like teenagers after a drunk night of partying, the ladies dived into the meal, forgetting all about the diets they were on.

"Ok. Ok. Let's playyyyy…. *Never have I.* I'll go first. Imma announce something that I've NEVER done, something outrageous, and if you've done that before, you have to take a shot. Ok ummmmmm…… NEVER have I……. fucked in my parents' bed." Neysa blurted out, leaving the other girls laughing.

Her eyes searched each friend as she waited for one of them to grab a shot glass. Nobody spoke; they all looked at each other smiling, clearly tipsy already.

"Ok fuck it. It was one time when my parents went to Canada and…."

"Ahhhhh Dallas, why are we NOT surprised?" Shonnie cut her off mid-sentence and asked while Neysa spotted Trinity out the corner of her eye, knocking back her glass.

"Ohhhh bitch, you not slick. Trinity a nasty ass hoe too." Neysa stood up and yelled, pointing her finger in Trinity's face.

The room erupted in laughter as Trinity playfully kicked Neysa, never once connecting, but somehow, she fell back on her ass anyway. Rubbing her lower back, which she hit on the table, Neysa crawled back to her feet before flopping back down on the couch.

"She knows damn well she ain't no drinker. Why we let her take all those shots?" Neysa heard Dallas fuss in her left ear while Shonnie agreed in the right.

It was true, whenever Neysa got drunk, she became a different person, a person only her girls could control. To the outside world, she was Dr. Brown, but with tequila in her system, there was no telling who you might get.

CHAPTER NINE

Dallas held the pistol in her hand and smiled as she stared down her target. Squeezing the trigger, she made sure not to close her eyes like the many times before. Fingering the piece of cold steel, Dallas released, firing shots after shots.

"Good job, baby. Next time, aim for the nigga head." Chinks cheered on from behind as they examined the damages on the white sheet of paper.

It was date night for the Moores at one of their favorite spots, George's Gun Range. With the busy flow at the shop and Chinks many many business adventures, they hadn't been on an official date in months.

"When we leave here, can we stop at Cold Stone? I got a taste for some ice cream," Dallas requested as Chinks prepped for his round.

"Yeah, that's cool. I gotta stop and holler at Ocean about something when…."

"Chinks, you said absolutely no business tonight." Dallas interrupted him and stated, placing her hands on her hips.

"It ain't business, I'm going to holler at my brother about…."

"BUSINESS! You act like I'm slow." She snapped, rolling her eyes and walking away, giving him space to fire his weapon.

"Listen." Chinks paused and checked the clip.

"We.... Not.... Gon'.... Be.... Long!" he assured her while letting off shots after each word.

Smacking her lips loudly, Dallas folded her arms across her chest and pouted until he was done. She didn't mind him stopping by to holler at Ocean; it was the principal and the fact he failed to keep his word. Chinks had been hustling his whole life, which was half the time they've been together. Raised by a single father, it was impossible for him not to follow his dad's hustling ass ways. Ronny wasn't a kingpin; however, he wasn't a nickel and dime man either. He did what he had to do to make sure his only child ate. Taking notes all his life, Chinks applied everything he was taught and became that kingpin Ronny wasn't able to be.

"Man, fix yo face and come on." Chinks barked, snapping Dallas out of her daze but not her attitude.

Dragging her feet, they headed to the front to return the equipment, so they could leave. Once they made it outside, Dallas continued her slow stride, only to piss him off, like he was doing her.

"Imma go in the morning to grab those slabs of ribs. You still making lasagna, right?"

Dallas's eyes rolled deep in the back of her head as her husband held a conversation with himself. Maybe from the outside looking in, she seemed petty or even childish, but she had her reasons and the opinions from others didn't matter.

"Dallas Renee Moore, stop fucking ignoring me!" Chinks looked over at her from the driver's side and cursed, his jawbone clenching tightly.

"Dallas Renee Moore TOWNSEND." She corrected and reminded him like she always did, insuring he remembered her maiden name.

"But yes, I'm making the lasagna. Any more questions?" she sassily asked, turning in her seat to face him.

Dallas watched as Chink smiled and shook his head from side to side. She knew he was only doing that to keep his cool. Unlike Dallas, Chinks hated arguing, so he calmed himself down inside his head.

"And then to top it off…."

I needed some shit with some bop in it (let's go)

I flew past the whip with that blunt in my mouth

Watch the swervin', that whip had a cop in it (woo)

My bitch got good pussy, fly her 'cross the country

I finish the show and I hop in it

"I KNOW YOU FUCKN' LYING. DON'T TURN NO MUSIC UP ON ME WHEN I'M TALKING!" Dallas yelled banging her fist on the dashboard of the car.

With each turn of the volume knob, Dallas's anger grew more and more, ready to punch him in his shit at that moment.

"Dallas, you put yo hands on me and Imma choke a bugga out yo ass." He threatened, never once taking his eyes off the road.

Balling up her fist tighter, Dallas stared out the window, trying to control her temper. The night that she had been looking forward to was now ruined, and she was ready to go home. With her face screwed and attitude on one hundred, Dallas remained quiet.

Pulling behind Ocean's car in the driveway, Dallas unbuckled her seatbelt and exited the whip before Chinks could switch gears. Storming up their walkway in her Air

Max 95s, Dallas skipped up the few steps before ringing the bell. Turning around, she spotted Chinks' bowlegged ass strutting up towards her. Frowning her face at the sight of him, Dallas turned back around, only to hear Chinks laughing behind her. Just as she was about to address him, the door swung open and Ocean's six-foot something frame stood there, guarded.

"Move! Where my friend?" she pushed passed him rudely and asked, forcing her way inside the house.

"The fuck wrong with her?" Dallas heard Ocean ask before finding Neysa laid out on the couch.

"I thought it was date night. What you doing here?" she sat up and asked, clearly surprised by the visit.

"I thought so too. What you watching?" Dallas questioned, pushing Neysa's feet to the side so she could take a seat.

Flopping down on the couch, Dallas began to untie her shoes in order to ger comfortable. Sure, Chinks said that it wouldn't be long, but she'll be a fool to believe that. Chinks and Ocean was just as tight as Dallas and Neysa; they were the reason they became friends in the first place. Tied to the hip since pampers, both Chinks and Ocean ran one of the most lucrative drug businesses in the Midwest.

“Yo ass still sitting around with an attitude. Why the fuck you take yo shoes off?” Chinks entered the living room and asked, shaking his head at the sight of his wife.

“Chinks don’t worry about me. Take care of yo “business” so I can go home.” Dallas snapped, cutting her eyes at him and then back at the television.

“Aye bro. Let’s go downstairs.” Ocean chimed in, trying to deescalate the situation, heading towards the stairs with Chinks in tow.

With the tv now on mute, the women remained quiet until they heard music coming from the basement. Now turning in her seat to face Neysa, Dallas pulled out her phone and began to scroll.

“So, what y’all have planned for tonight?” Dallas asked as she accepted a few friend requests on Facebook.

“Shit. I was gon’ chill since this my last weekend for I go back to work. Why? What’s up?” Neysa’s perfectly arched eyebrow raised high in the air.

“Well as you can see, my night didn’t go as planned, but I ain’t trying to be in the house either.” Dallas told her, stopping on a picture of Trinity.

"Aye Neysa, have you heard from Trinity since Shonnie left?" she quizzed, befriending her and scrolling through her post.

Hearting pictures as she goes, Dallas noticed how Trinity was a private person versus the social media guru she took her as.

"Nope, I'm about to text her now. Maybe she got plans for us since yo lame ass don't."

Throwing a decorative pillow at her head, Dallas left Neysa to do that while she moved over to Instagram where she headed to the ShadeRoom. Laughing at some of the ridiculous things they posted, she was still addicted to the celebrity gossip blog page.

"She said she's at home …. BUT…. we can come over and watch fireworks from her rooftop…. In the pool." Neysa said, interrupting Dallas and her trolling.

"Damn… straight up! Wait. I ain't got nun to swim in." Dallas excitement declined, remembering she wasn't close to home.

"Girl, I got like seven I ain't never wore. Come on." Neysa stood to her feet and stated, walking up the stairs to her bedroom.

"I mean, it's a medium and that ass of yours is an EXTRA LARGE, but I meannnnn, we can work with it." Neysa continued talking shit as thoughts of tripping her up the stairs plagued Dallas's mind.

After fifteen minutes of changing clothes and getting their hair just right, Dallas and Neysa was out the front door and headed to Trinity's place.

"Aye. Did you tell Chinks you were gone?" Neysa turned to Dallas and asked, pulling the seatbelt across her chest.

"Girl, fuck him. That nigga will be here when we get back. Let's go!"

CHAPTER TEN

It had been a month and a half since Trinity made that transition back to her hometown, Chicago. Pretty much, nothing had changed, especially seeing how she visited so often when she was away. Catching up with old friends and spending time with her aunt had been the highlight for her thus far. Slightly disappointed that Shonnie was miles away, Trinity still enjoyed the time that she spent with her new girlfriends, Dallas and Neysa. Off bat, there seemed to be a connection between her and the other ladies and the vibe they gave off was good. Neysa was reserved until she got drunk, and Dallas was a hot girl, twenty-four-seven.

"Imma head out Auntie. I'll call you when I leave the barbeque." Trinity yelled through her aunt's apartment, heading towards the front door.

"Wait, girl." Aunt Shelia huffed and puffed as she rushed out of the backroom, trying to catch her niece before she left.

Stopping in her tracks, Trinity took a deep breath before slowly turning around, facing her favorite person in the world.

"I got a call yesterday from a 212 area code, don't…."

"Auntie, don't worry about it. I promise I got everything under control. Now you gon' make me late. I'll see you later." Trinity cut her off mid-sentence and silenced her with a kiss on the cheek.

She loved her TeeTee, but her and that gift of gab never seemed to stop going. Glancing down at the time on her phone's screen, Trinity picked up the pace and powerwalked to her car. It was almost eight and Dallas's 4th of July barbeque started at six, almost two hours ago. In her defense, it wasn't completely her fault. Her beautician, Lakia, was eight months pregnant, but instead of being on bedrest, she was chasing a bag and taking a break every three minutes.

Go figure
You were the trigger
You brought me to an obstructed view
When you knew the picture was bigger
Who am I kiddin'?
Knew from the beginning
You'd ruin everything, you do it every time
You are my enemy, you are no friend of mind, muhfucker

Turning up the volume in her Jag to the max, Trinity flipped down the Gucci shades that rested on her head before driving off in the sunset. Pissed that she was late but excited that she was invited, Trinity couldn't wait to vibe with good people and listen to even better music. Using her signal to merge in the right lane, she prepared to make her exit, which was less than a mile away. A few blocks from the expressway, Trinity doubled checked the address to make sure she was out front.

"Damn… this muthafucker nice!" she admired loudly as she struggled to find a park.

Telling from the amount of cars lined along the street, it was clear that Dallas's backyard fiesta was lit. Flipping down the sun visor, Trinity applied another coat of lip gloss and fixed her edges before grabbing her purse and exiting the car.

Dressed in a long peach flowy maxi dress that she snugged from Nordstrom and a pair of comfortable sandals from Aldo. Trinity strutted across the street, following the sound of 90s R&B into the packed backyard. Instantly recognizing a few faces, mostly from high school, she gave off a warm smile to each before locking eyes with Dallas. Thinking back to the first night when she saw her at the club, those same juices began to flow between her legs.

Regretting not wearing any panties, Trinity walked over to Dallas with sticky thoughts between her thighs.

"Hey baby, I didn't think you would make it." Dallas greeted her with a huge smile and hug the moment they were face to face.

"Hey girl. I'm sorry for being late. You have a lovely backyard." Trinity replied, looking around, impressed with the layout.

"I'm ready for something bigger. Come on, let me show you around."

Starting with the kitchen, Dallas gave Trinity a complete tour, including the upstairs bedrooms. Making the final stop in the basement, Trini followed Dallas down a set of stairs into a smoke-filled room.

"Crack a fucking window in here. Sheesh!" Dallas fussed, fanning with her hands as they made it to the other side of the basement.

"Aye y'all. Y'all remember Trinity? Trinity, this my husband Chinks. You know Neysa's bald-headed ass. This her bodyguard looking ass nigga Ocean… annnnndddddd that's Nick, Jaz, Trey, and Kenny over there."

Speaking and giving each and every one of them eye contact, Trinity felt a little at ease, seeing how everyone was so welcoming. Heading back up the stairs with Dallas and Neysa joining them, they returned to the backyard where they sat at an empty table.

"This was a really nice turn out." Neysa spoke first, glancing around as more people joined the party.

"Girl, I told Chinks this the last year we having this shit here."

"And you said that same shit last year, Dallas." Neysa checked, causing Trinity to laugh at her bluntness.

Replying with a middle finger, the ladies shared another laugh before Chinks walked up with a bottle of Patron.

"We gon' start the fireworks in a few bae." He announced, placing a kiss on Dallas's full lips.

"Looks like this nigga trying to get you drunk." Neysa pointed out, grabbing the liquor and pouring each of them a cup.

"Looks like he ain't the only one." Trinity laughed, grabbing the cup from Neysa, preparing to down the straight liquor.

"To fireworks, Independence, and friendships!" Dallas held her cup high in the air and yelled, drawing eyes from across the yard.

Following right behind her, Trinity and Neysa repeated those exact words in unison before toasting to a promising night. It seemed as if the drinks never stopped after the first shot and after her third cup, Trinity had lost count. Remembering fireworks and footworking in the middle of the lawn but everything else in between was a blur, Trinity had officially reached her limit; however, that was a few drinks ago.

"Da-Da-Dallas, you better make sure those people outta yo house." Neysa's words slurred as she collapsed on the sectional couch in the living room.

"Get yo drunk ass off of me heifer." Dallas fought, pushing Neysa to the ground, causing them all to laugh.

"You hoes drunk." Dallas continued, now helping her best friend off the floor.

"I ain't drunk. I'm decent but not drunk." Trinity semi-lied, searching the cracks of the couch, attempting to find her phone.

She could look at Dallas and tell that she was slightly tipsy, but Neysa, on the other hand, was fucked up.

"You know what friend? Tomorrow, I'm going to come get a tattoo and----"

"Yup! That's her cue to go. OCEAN! Come take yo woman home!" Dallas yelled out to the kitchen where the guys gathered and talked shit.

Laughing but a bit confused, Trinity sat and watched on as Dallas kicked Neysa out of her house.

"Whenever she gets drunk, she wants to get a tattoo. It never fails. Every fucking time." Dallas explained from her spot on the couch.

"Ohhhh, so that's her drunk signal." Trinity confirmed, trying to control her laughter.

"I'm supposed to be her best friend, and I can't even get a tattoo outta the bitch. Lil light skin hoe!" Neysa cursed, now sitting Indian style in the middle of the floor.

"Now Dallas, why won't you tat her?" Trinity turned to her and instigated with a straight face.

"Fuck you Trinity, cuz you can leave too." Dallas cursed at her now, causing her to curl up in a ball giggling.

"I'm not about to play with you or Neysa." Dallas threatened, pointing her fingers at the both of them before continuing.

"I get my rocks off by tattooing newbies, and since my BFF over here is ink free, I've been trying to take her ink virginity for years."

"And I refuse to end up looking like you." Neysa shouted, finally standing to her feet.

Trinity smiled and wished to have a friendship as tight as theirs. Shonnie was the closest friend to it, but their distance kept them from forming that perfect bond. Looking over at Dallas, Trinity's eyes undressed her, imaging what her tattoos looked like underneath her clothes.

Short in height but stacked everywhere else, Dallas had the body of a fitness trainer but the ass of your favorite Instagram model. Tattoos covered her light skin; it seemed as if they were everywhere but her face and chest. Licking her lips, Trinity's eyes traveled back up to Dallas's face, just as she looked over at her.

"Trinity, you good over there?" She asked, noticing the seductive look on her now embarrassed face.

"Aw nah. I was just thinking. I'm a virgin. You can ink fuck me." Trinity recovered perfectly, showing off her bare skin.

"SWEAR TO GOD! YOU HAVE NOT ONE TAT?" Dallas eagerly said, rushing over, scanning Trinity's body.

"Nope. Not one. I guess I'll schedule an appointment first thing Monday morning." She replied, sitting back on the sofa.

"MONDAY? Gurl stop, I can do it right now in my tattoo dungeon. Come on!" Dallas ordered, pulling Trinity up and away from the everyone else.

"Okayyyyy… So, what you wanna get? Something small orrrrr BIG? As a matter of fact, this shit is art, you need to think about it?" Dallas asked, leading her to a large room in the back of their basement.

During the tour, they never made it pass the weed smoke, so Trinity hadn't seen that room or another closed door in the cut. The inside of Dallas's ink dungeon resembled a miniature tattoo shop. She had all the tools and supplies, including a little rose gold register off in the corner. Trinity could tell that tattooing was Dallas's passion, just from the way her eyes lit up when someone mentioned the word.

"I know what I want already." Trinity advised while Dallas handed her folders full of artwork.

"Oh okay. I'm listening." She smiled, grabbing a sheet of paper and pen.

Trinity took a deep breath and closed her eyes as flashbacks of August 29th invaded her thoughts. It was the one day that she'll never forget, yet the only day she wished she could completely erase. August 29th, she gave birth, birth to a still born.

"I want Roman numerals, right here." Trinity instructed, pointing to her inner right wrist where Dallas's soft hands glided over the small veins.

"Dope. What's the number?" Dallas asked her as she placed on a pair of latex gloves.

"August 29th, 2019." Trinity softly replied.

Without any questioning behind the reason, Dallas gathered further detail from Trinity regarding the design before prepping the area for the drawing. Taking deep breathes in and out, Trinity tried to control her anxiety, but nothing seemed to work. She wasn't a fan of pain and the sound from Dallas testing the needle drove her insane.

"Wait. Can we take a shot before you get started?" Trinity contested, standing to her feet and walking over to the table where they placed their drinks.

"Cool!" Dallas quickly agreed, removing one glove and joining Trinity.

Unable to recall how many shots or cups they've had, both women figured that one more wouldn't hurt, so they gulped down last of the dark liquor. Instantly feeling the burn, Trinity felt a rush as well the Henny had given her the adrenaline she needed to proceed with the tattoo.

"Whew, chile!" Dallas grimaced, apparently feeling the same way Trinity felt, which in Trinity's eyes was a good thing.

"Aight D. Let's get this shit over with. You say it's not gon' hurt, but I know you lying." Trinity fussed walking back over, taking a seat in the hot pink leather chair.

"It's not. I swear it's like losing yo virginity for real. Once the pain resides, the shit start to feel good." Dallas replied, trying to comfort her.

It didn't help much, but Trinity appreciated the effort from her new friend. She couldn't believe she was getting a tattoo, the moment seemed surreal. If her Aunt Shelia knew what she was doing, she'll have a heart attack. "*Marking up God's work*" is what she'll call it, and Trini dreaded the moment she found out.

“I’m ready. I’m ready.” She hyped herself, relaxing her mind first and then her body followed after.

The entire session lasted about forty-five minutes, and Trinity couldn’t have been happier when it was over. The pain was mediocre, the dreadful stories she’s heard from others was no worse than the actual experience itself. Once Dallas shaded the letters in, her skin became numb, so numb that it no longer bothered her.

“It’s soooo dope, Dallas. Thank you so much.” Trinity babbled, loving how the red ink looked against her golden skin.

“You’re welcome girl. I told you my pussy get wet from fresh skin and ….”

“Let me see.” Trinity unknowingly blurted out, immediately kicking herself in the ass afterwards.

Unsure if Dallas had heard her or not, Trinity remained quiet a few more seconds, testing the vibe in the room.

“What you wanna see, Trinity?” Dallas turned to her and questioned, slowly walking back over towards her in the chair.

Dallas towered over Trinity, her crouch at eye level, only tempting her even more. Flirting amongst the two had been innocent, well at least up until this point. Trinity was well aware of the lifestyle Dallas lived, but she assumed it was only when her husband was included. She had never heard of stories involving Dallas being one on one with a woman, which only made her even more curious.

"What you wanna see, Trinity?"

"This?"

Dallas took Trinity's hand and placed it between her legs, where Trini instantly felt how wet she was through the leggings she wore. Her pussy being fatter than Trinity had imagined made her only want her even more.

"You sure we should…."

"Shhhhhh…. Play with it." Dallas ordered and just like an obedient servant, Trinity did as she was told.

Placing her hands inside of Dallas's leggings, Trinity played with her swollen clit, causing soft moans to escape from her lips. Speeding up the pace, Dallas tossed her head back, displaying that she was enjoying the feeling.

"You lay here. I wanna eat yo pussy." Trinity requested, removing her hands and standing to her feet.

Dallas took a few steps back before stepping out of her clothes while Trinity admired the way her body looked. Unable to hold out any longer, Trinity walked over to

Dallas and kissed her, easing her tongue inside her mouth. Engaging in a passionate kiss for a few seconds, Trinity stepped away before guiding Dallas over to the chair.

"Sit down and open up."

With her legs wide in the air, Trinity wasted no time, diving in between them, getting her first taste of Mrs. Dallas Moore.

"Damn, girl!" Dallas moaned, lifting up to get a better view of Trinity's head as it roamed freely in between her legs.

Hearing her and knowing that Dallas was being pleased turned Trinity on even more. Geeked and now inspired, Trini put on her best performance, ultimately, getting the results she wanted. Dallas's moans became louder and louder, putting Trinity in a zone--a zone where she tuned everything out, everything expect the moans. With her eyes closed and tongue going to work, Trinity paused when she felt a pair of hands on her waist.

"My bad Trinity, is it okay for Chinks to join us?"

Trinity's eyes shifted back and forth between Dallas, who laid in the chair and her husband who stood behind her with his dick in his hands. At almost thirty,

Trinity had never experienced a threesome, yet, it was something on her bucket list.

"Bend over. Finish eating her pussy." Chinks' deep voice ordered as he lifted Trinity's dress, spreading her ass cheeks.

The room began to spin, putting her in a daze, but somehow, she still knew exactly what she was doing when she arched her back and began to throw it back. Chinks thick dick rammed inside her pussy as she devoured Dallas's. Unsure of how long their sexapade lasted, Trinity woke up the next morning, fully clothed, laid across their couch with a slight headache. Scared to open her eyes but even more afraid to face reality, she stayed put. Laying still, playing possum, Trinity thought of ways she could dip out unnoticed and keep the little dignity that she still had.

CHAPTER ELEVEN

Day 1 was in the books and Neysa regretted not taking a longer vacation. Sure, she was relaxed since most of the time was spent on her ass. Her and Ocean still hadn't managed to get anything done, and like always, he blamed it on her and her busy work schedule.

"Quit, Neysa. You set for life."

Ocean's voice echoed through her head as she prepared to leave for the day. Logging out of all the systems, Neysa grabbed her Nike bookbag and strolled to the elevator. Smiling on the inside, the moment the doors immediately opened, Neysa stepped forward behind them.

"Excuse me." She glanced up and smiled at the gentleman already inside.

"Wait. You going up or down?" she said aloud, noticing that elevator cart was headed up.

"I'm going wherever you going." She heard a deep voice say from behind her.

"WHAT!" She frowned, smacking her lips and turning around to face the clown.

Slick comebacks and rebuttals were brewing in her head; however, none of it made it to surface when she laid eyes on him.

"I-I- I said up or down." She stuttered before clearing her throat and fixing her smock.

His stares made her feel uneasy, so uncomfortable that she turned back around and allowed the elevator to do its thing. Finally stopping at the tenth floor, the doors open, but no one got off.

"This yo floor, ain't it?" Neysa turned and asked her guest who said nothing but instead smiled.

Standing at about six-foot one, a little shorter than she preferred, Neysa's elevator guest looks made up for whatever he lacked in height. Dark in tone with a deep wave fade, he was beyond attractive and the way his eyes was piercing her soul made Neysa weak.

"I told you, I'm going where you going." He repeated, reaching across her and pressing the buttons to close the doors.

"This nigga better gonnnneeee…" she whispered under her breath, shaking her head from side to side.

Neysa got hit on daily everywhere she went, especially at work. Seeing a young, black, fly ass doctor, for some reason, drove them insane, men and women.

Looking him up and down, Neysa prayed they arrived on the ground level soon. It was a lot of tension on the elevator, and she needed fresh air, expeditiously.

"So, doc. Look right. I been coughing and shit and…"

"You need to schedule an appointment." Neysa cut him off, just at the sound of the elevator bells.

"But what if I fall out in this bitch right now? You took some type of oath or sum, right? You gotta save me." He followed behind her out into the parking garage.

Chuckling to herself, Neysa focused forward, hoping he get the picture before it's too late. Ocean was waiting out front to pick her up, and if Mr. Elevator Guest knew like she knew, he'll go about his business.

"Look sweetheart, if you need assistance, you can take the elevator back to the main level. If it is an emergency, call 9-1-1. Have a blessed day." Neysa told him with a fake smile, her eyes shifting back to Ocean, who was now getting out the car.

The palm of her hands became sweaty as thoughts of how things were going to play-out ran through her mind. Outside of Ocean being a big nigga, his entire demeanor was intimidating, even to some of the toughest men on Earth.

"I guess that's yo nigga right there, dodging cars and shit, trying to get over here." He paused, chuckling and pointing at Ocean while he held up traffic.

"Imma let you go before buddy's ass end up on a stretcher and then you mad at me for killing the nigga and now you won't let me take you out." he continued, causing Neysa to laugh.

"You have a good day." She smiled one last time before turning on her heels and walking away.

"You too, Dr. N. Brown!" he yelled out from behind her, just as she met Ocean at the curb.

"WHO THE FUCK WAS THAT NIGGA?" he barked, trying to step forward, but Neysa stopped him.

"A family member of a patient. Chill.... The fuck?" Neysa cursed, adjusting her bookbag and heading to the car.

When they first started dating, Neysa thought Ocean and his controlling ways was cute; fast forward almost fifteen years later and now it turns her stomach. In her opinion, they were too old for the shit, and instead of establishing trust, Ocean was ready to kill any man that looked her way. And although infidelity never played a major role in their relationship, you'll think she cheated with every Tom, Dick and Harry, the way Ocean acted.

"I gotta make a stop to check on the count then we can head to the crib."

The sound of his voice triggered a deep eye roll, followed by her smacking her lips. Neysa had just worked twelve hours and the last thing she wanted to do was ride around the hood.

"I gotta use it. Drop me off at the shop around the corner." She requested, putting her seatbelt on and adjusting her ass in the leather seats.

Without saying a word, Ocean did as he was told, pulling inside the parking lot of a strip mall and finding a park.

"How long its gon' take you to do what you gotta do?" Neysa turned to him and asked as she reached for the door handle.

"Ten minutes max baby." Ocean turned to her and replied, his deep brown eyes staring into hers.

"I'll stay here. Hurry up. Be careful." She told him before he leaned in, placing a soft but yet juicy kiss on her lips.

Feeling her pussy tingle a bit, Neysa sucked on his bottom lip before ending their make out session and exiting the ride. The sun beaming down on her chocolate skin, Neysa fixed her baby hairs before entering the nail shop.

"NEYSA! NEYSA! NEYSA!" Everyone yelled out her name in heavy Korean accents as they worked on the women in their chairs.

"Hey y'all!" she spoke, waving her hands high in the air before walking around the first station.

"Hey Appa!" *(Dad in Korean)* Neysa smiled, hugging her father and owner of N&N Nails and Spas.

Having a Korean stepfather had always been a blessing and a curse for her, especially growing up. Neysa and Lee Sui had a great relationship when she was younger; however, it changed after she started dating Ocean. Blaming it on her mom Pam, Neysa knew her opinion of Ocean rubbed off on Lee.

"What do I owe the visit, seeing how last time I seen you, you were –"

"Dad, could we not. Not right now. Not in here." Neysa pleaded, shaking her head slowly from side to side.

She knew where that conversation was going, and she had no plans on visiting there. The last time she spoke to either parent was at her nephew's party, and although she felt bad for disrespecting her dad, she regretted nothing regarding her mom.

"Ok Princess, you're right. How you been?" He asked her before sitting, leading the way to the back.

"Good. I'm been good. Vacation over, headaches from adjusting to being a new doctor, but I guess that's what I signed up for, right?" she shrugged, taking a seat on the couch in the employee's lounge.

"Well you worked hard for sure, and both me and your mother are proud of you." He spoke softly, his wrinkled skin, smiling from ear to ear.

"Yeah. Yeah. Yeah. I gotta pee. I'll be back." Neysa dismissed him and all the bullshit he was kicking about them being proud of her.

She knew how they felt, especially since they were so vocal about it. After she relieved herself and washed her hands, Neysa went to tell her dad goodbye. She rathered wait in the hot sun for Ocean than to be lectured by him.

"I'm gone, Appa. I'll give you a call later." She lied, ducking her head in and out of the room, thinking she got away safe.

"Wait. Come here." He yelled, stopping her dead in her tracks.

Cursing to herself, Neysa turned around and eased her way back towards him, just as Ocean sent her a text.

"What's up?" she causally asked, praying that he wouldn't be long.

"In all honesty, we are proud of you, regardless of what you may think. Yes, we are disappointed in some of the choices you've made in life and the people you've made them with, but we still love you. We just hate that you almost risked it all for a fucking loser." Lee spat, his last comment catching Neysa off guard.

Chuckling to herself, Neysa was actually speechless, especially at how the whole speech played out. Just when she thought things was sweet, the slanted eyed man hit her with a curve ball.

"We love you and don't wanna see you throw your career away, but most importantly, your life for a boy who can't grow up." He blurted out just before she was fully gone.

On a regular day, her father and his words would have hurt her, but sadly, Neysa was used to it. Her parents had no reason to dislike him, and if anyone was to blame, it was her. Neysa's love for her man ran deep and it showed.

"What's wrong? Why you looking like that?" Ocean questioned the moment she stepped foot in the car.

"Nun. I'm good. Was the count and everything straight?" She asked, making a mental note to control her facial expressions better.

She knew she had to change the subject in order to keep Ocean calm. There was no way in the world she was repeating what her father said, especially when they were still parked out front.

"Yeah, the shit was cool." He replied, giving her the side eye as if he knew she was lying.

"As a matter of fact, I talked to the niggas at the warehouse, and we running low on pills and drank, it's about time we re-up." He stated, backing out of the parking spot and heading in the direction of their house.

"I kinda figured it was time. I'll grab some more scripts when I go in tomorrow, but I restocked the safe with that other shit. We should be good on that for a while if we distribute what we already have." Neysa explained to him from the passenger's seat of his Benz.

Without saying another word, Ocean shook his head up and down before turning up the music and hitting Lake Shore Drive. Neysa knew he loved when she took control, so that's what she always did. By day, she was a doctor, but by night, she was a trap queen; risking it all for the man she loved.

CHAPTER TWELVE

"I'll like a mimosa anddddd a veggie omelet please." Dallas smiled as she handed the waitress the menu.

"And let me get the same. Thank you, sweetheart." Neysa beamed before turning to face her friend.

Smiling from ear to ear, both ladies stared at each other until they were left alone.

"Okay bitch, now tell me EVERYTHING and don't leave nothing out." Neysa said, making Dallas laugh out aloud at her eagerness.

Sunday brunches was their new thing, especially when they needed to catch up and a phone call wasn't good enough. It had only been a few days since her backyard boogie on Independence Day, and although they spoke every day, Dallas hadn't told Neysa everything that happened after she left.

Starting from the top, Dallas gave her best friend play by play details regarding the threesome involving Trinity. Neysa's mouth was wide open as she listened to the detailed events. Dallas cringed herself as the words left her mouth. She sounded like a freak and anybody listening would think the same.

"Wait, so y'all went upstairs and…."

"Save all questions for the end." Dallas told her before finishing the story.

By the time she was done, they were on their second mimosa and their food had arrived.

"Have you talked to Shonnie?" Dallas asked before placing a fork full of eggs inside her mouth.

"Not since last night. Her plane landed an hour ago. I told her to meet us here but…."

"Speaking of the devil." Dallas cut her off and stated, pointing through the glass window as Shonnie got out of her car.

"And look who she brought with her…. HMPH! Trinnnniiitttyyyyyy!" Neysa teased like a kid on the playground.

Laughing before taking a sip from her cup, Dallas watched as both women made their way inside the establishment. Her eyes specifically glued on Trinity who wore a pair of short shorts, a cream blazer, her breast sitting up perfectly underneath, and a pair of red leather pumps.

"Here come yo little girlfrienddddddd." Neysa bubbled, laughing at her own childish behavior.

Sticking up her middle finger, Dallas turned back around, just as they approached the table. Happy to see

Shonnie and even more happy that she was home two weeks early, both Dalla and Neysa stood to their feet, greeting Shonnie and Trinity.

"We ordered omelets since we were starving. Y'all want anything?" Dallas asked, ready to flag down their waitress.

"Just drinks for me. I ate at the airport." Shonnie explained.

"And I'm fasting. I'll get a glass of water." Trinity told them just as the waiter arrived back at the table.

Once all the orders were taken, Shonnie filled the gang in on her trip and why it was cut short. With the summer coming to an end, Dallas was excited that they were going to be spending the last days of it together. Leo season was approaching, so she was ready to cut up for her birthday month and see needed her team with her.

"So, D. I'm still pissed I missed the 4th at your house. I bet it was lit." Shonnie turned to Dallas and said as both Neysa and Trinity's eyes landed on her, awaiting a response.

"It was lit friend. I wish you was there.'' Dallas replied, keeping it short and sweet.

Dallas wasn't sure if Trinity told Shonnie or not, therefore, she played it safe. Outside of Neysa, no one else knew about them, and she was perfectly fine keeping it that way. Secrets were not something that their clique kept, so Dallas knew Shonnie would know sooner or later.

"So, Dallas, I seen on Facebook... Yo birthday coming up. What you got planned?" Trinity questioned, changing the subject and shifting the mood at the table.

'You know what? I was thinking about doing something cute and simple this year. I wanna save all my energy for when I turn thirty." She explained, still unsure of any exact plans herself.

Usually, Chinks would go all out with celebrating, but she told him the same, cute and simple until she decides elsewise. Talks about birthdays, relationships, cooking recipes, and more filled the air as the women filled their belly with bottomless mimosas.

"Aye Trinity, ain't that Aunt Shelia right there?" Dallas heard Shonnie's voice say, causing her to look from her phone.

Dallas watched as an older woman waltzed her way over to them with a huge smile planted on her chubby face.

From first glance, she would have assumed that she was Trinity's mom, their resemblance was uncanny.

"Heyyyy girrlllllllsssss…" she spoke, distributing a warm smile to each of them.

"Ladies, this is my Aunt Shelia. Auntie, this is Neysa, Dallas and you already know Shonnie. I went to high school with them too." Trinity explained, ensuring that everyone was acquainted.

Trinity's aunt stood around making small talk with them until her table was ready. It was now noon and the special guest DJ was now spinning the latest rap and R&B records. The once quiet place quickly turned into a day party, making it hard for Dallas to leave.

"I gotta head out to take care of some business y'all." Dallas stood to her feet and abruptly said, grabbing her Louie bag and easing out.

She lost track of time and hated being late, regardless if it was something big or small. Forgetting to mention the leave to Neysa earlier, Dallas decided to shoot her a text in the car instead. Hugging and kissing cheeks with each girl before she left, Dallas dropped a hundred-dollar bill on the table before dashing out.

Glancing down at the gold Rolex that rested on her wrist, Dallas calmed down a bit, noticing that she actually had more time than she thought. Walking much slower now, she fixed her wig and fanned her face before reaching her car.

Bringing the coupe to life, Dallas dropped the top on her Benz, adjusted her oversized Chanel glasses on her face, and headed downtown to Michigan Avenue. With it being early on a Sunday, traffic was light, and Dallas loved it. The breeze from the lake was mild, making it seem cooler than it really was.

Arriving with ten minutes to spare, Dallas valet parked her car and headed inside to get a jump start on paperwork. Walking through the empty lobby, her heels clicking on the marble floor, Dallas took the elevator to the twenty-seventh floor. Walking down a long hallway, full of different offices and businesses, she could only imagine how packed the place would be on a weekday. Thankful for the opportunity, Dallas said a silent prayer before opening a set of glass doors with the words:

Dr. T. Turner, MD, OB/GYN, DSN,

“Good evening ma’am. How can I help you?” a petite middle-aged white woman greeted her from behind a small receptionist desk.

“Yes, I am here to see Dr. Turner. My name is Dallas Moore. I’m her one o ‘clock.” She replied, pulling her ID out of her wallet.

“Oh yes. You’re her last patient. Fill out the information on this clipboard, and I’ll let her know you’re here.”

Doing as she was told, Dallas filled out the new patient questionnaire in record time. Being as impatient as she was, she knew how doctors operated. They’ll schedule six people; ten minutes apart and still be an hour late arriving.

“Mrs. Moore, when you’re done, the doctor is ready to see you.” Becky called out in the empty waiting area.

Standing to her feet, Dallas returned the clipboard along with her insurance information before being led away to the back.

“Since this is a consultation, we won’t need any blood work from you just yet. Dr. Turner will be right in with you.” She assured Dallas who took a seat in the leather chair across from the desk.

Grabbing her phone from her bag, Dallas scrolled Facebook and Instagram to pass time. A feeling of sorrow overcame her as social media continued to mourn the untimely death of NBA great, Kobe Bryant. Her heart still ached for his wife who lost not only her husband but her daughter as well. Life was truly too short, that's why Dallas planned on living hers to the fullest.

"Hey Mrs. Moore. I'm Dr. Turner, how are you?" an older black woman entered the room wearing a pencil skirt, blouse, and white long smock asked.

"I'm great. How are you?" Dallas questioned with a smile as she took a seat behind the desk.

Dallas heard nothing but good things about Dr. Turner, and after doing her own research, she realized she was the best person for the job. On top of having amazing credentials, Dallas's heart smiled when she learned that it was a black woman who owned her own clinic. After pulling a few strings and spending a couple of dollars, she was finally able to get an appointment with the best fertility doctor in the Chicagoland.

CHAPTER THIRTEEN

Trinity jumped up at the alarming sound coming from the smoke detector and looked around her bedroom nervously. *Was the entire building on fire?* she wondered, especially since she lived alone, so she knew the smoke wasn't coming from her place.

"WHAT THE FUCK?" She yelled out, slipping on her slippers and pulling down the oversized T-shirt she wore.

Grabbing her phone and keys, just in case, Trinity hurried out of the bedroom, colliding with a cloud of smoke. Her worst thought was coming true. It was in fact her condo that was on fire, and she had no idea how that was possible. Fanning her hands wildly in the air, Trinity noticed that the sirens stopped, and the smoke thinned out. Calming down slightly, she inhaled deeply when the smell of burnt bacon captivated her nostrils.

Looking around for something to use as a weapon, Trinity crept into the kitchen empty handed, minus the belongings she took with her. Different thoughts and sceneries played through her mind as she tried to comb through the mystery. Why was the smell of bacon coming from her kitchen when no one knew where she lived?

Botham Jean, an unarmed black man who was killed in his own apartment by a white cop earlier in the year, became one of those thoughts. More scared now than ever, Trinity decided that making a dash for the door was smarter than trying to solve the case herself. Building up enough courage to run, Trinity's curiosity got the best of her, and she needed to know who was in her home. Peeking her head around the corner, her heart stopped at the sight of the home intruder, and unfortunately, it was too late to run.

"My bad shorty, I woke you up." Rico apologized from the stove as he poured pancake batter onto her grill.

"Wha- Wh- What the fuck? How you get in my house?" she stuttered, easing backwards towards the door.

"Damn baby. I thought you'll be happy to see me." He smiled, those deep dimples she once loved made her throw up in her mouth now.

Question after question skated through her mind, making it hard to choose which one to ask first. Thinking that it may possibly be a dream, Trinity thought of ways to wake up.

"I know you love ketchup on your eggs. Have a seat.'' He continued, placing the Henz ketchup on the table and then pulling the chair out for her.

"How you get in here? How you find me?" she finally mustarded up the strength to ask.

It was no secret; she was afraid of Rico. She knew the type of man he was and what he was capable of doing at any given time. Trying her best to play it safe, she plastered on a fake smile as she awaited an answer from him.

"Find you, huh? In order to find you, you must've went missing on purpose. Is that what it is?" he slowly walked closer to and quizzed.

Thinking about her next play, Trinity did what she should have done in the beginning and ran, except like last time, she didn't make it far. Rico grabbed a hand full of Trinity's braids, halting her attempt to the door. Grabbing her roots and hollering out in pain, Trinity stumbled back, landing on the kitchen floor. Quickly jumping back to her feet, she was taught to never allow anybody to kick her while she was down. She knew she couldn't beat Rico's ass, however, that never stopped her from trying before.

Regretting the night she met him four years ago at the Waffle House, Trinity deemed him as being ***the worst*** mistake in her life. Charmed by Rico's good looks and bad boy ways, he swept her off of her feet, only for her to land flat on her ass. Their first year together was magical; he was the man of her dreams and Trinity couldn't ask for more. Things began to shift when Rico started running the streets more. Quitting her job and going to school full time, Trinity began to lean on Rico more and that's when it hit the fan. He became controlling and overprotective; it was as if he was a new person.

"Why you wait until a nigga get locked up and fled the state? Did you not think Chicago would be the first place I looked?" he questioned, tilting his head to the side as Trinity stepped away.

"I told you it was over last year, Rico. It's not my fault you ain't let go." Trinity told him as tears began to stream down her face.

"LET GO! Bit-…. Trinity, you all I had, and you dipped out on a nigga the minute those people raided the crib." Rico explain, trying to control his anger.

"I was preparing for law school Rico. I had just got hired as a paralegal at the firm. What the fuck was I supposed to do? I mean, I wrote and visited you the first couple of months, but it became too much." She cried, this being the first face to face conversation the two had.

Rico was sentenced to two years and five months, and although that wasn't long, Trinity wasn't built for a jailhouse relationship. Sure, she loved Rico; however, at that stage in their relationship, she was no longer in love with him. Right before he got locked up, he became abusive and like most domestics, it started off verbally first.

On the night she got the call he was taken into custody, she immediately dropped to her knees and prayed. Trinity prayed that his sentencing would be the outlet she needed, but when she learned of the amount of time he got, she became devastated.

"So, you moved back here to be with *that* nigga?" Rico barked, the bass in his voice causing her to jump.

"NO. NO!" she yelled, now backing up into a wall as he approached her with nothing but hate in his eyes.

"You think I don't know about that nigga, Trinity? You think muthafuckers don't talk huh?" Rico asked her while she shriveled helpless in the corner.

Dying honestly crossed Trinity's thoughts. There was no question in her mind that Rico would kill her and not think twice about it. After Trini cut things off with him, he wrote her several letters explaining in horrific detail the things he'll do to her if she ever left him. Scared for her life, she fled, not thinking she'll be that easy to be found.

"You and that nigga was in love huh? Prancing around Atlanta like I ain't the mayor of that muthafucker. And look, what the fuck is this?" he asked, yanking her arm and examining the tattoo on her wrist.

"Awwww, this the date y'all baby died huh? I oughta cut this shit out yo skin right now. Guess you ain't know I knew about the pregnancy either.' He ranted, spit flying out of his mouth onto her chin.

"Rico, just go before I call the---"

Was the last words Trinity managed to get out before being choked until she passed out.

CHAPTER FOURTEEN

Using the side button on her phone to silence it, Neysa grabbed the patient's chart before entering the room. Greeting both parents with a smile, she introduced herself before getting down to business. It was a busy day at Oak Park Hospital and even busier in the Pediatrics unit where sick babies pilled in left and right. Without a break in her schedule, Neysa moved about her day as a robot, ensuring that everyone got the care that they deserved.

Finishing up with patient in the room, Dr. Brown issued a prescription for amoxicillin to treat an ear infection and moved on. Stopping at the receptionist desk, she grabbed a bottle of water and checked her phone. Several missed calls displayed from her parents with a new voicemail as well. Neysa had been ducking and dodging all their calls, especially since the run in at the nail shop. She was tired of hearing them voice their opinion about her and Ocean when she had everything under control. No one, not even Dallas, knew the role she played inside of Chink' and Ocean's organization. Keeping something like that from her best friend killed her, but she knew how disappointed Dallas would be, if she knew.

"Dr. Brown, your next patient is ready in room C. You have a Kayla Bishop annnndddd it's an annual checkup, everything up to date so this should be an easy one for you." Montana, her favorite nurse walked up and narrated.

"Thanks boo. Make sure you take yo break. Don't let this place kill you." Neysa told her before grabbing the chart out of her hands.

Speeding down the hall with the certain urge to pee, Neysa silenced her phone again as a call from her sister Nicole came through.

"Why the fuck they keep calling me?" she cursed under her breath, ignoring a call just as another one came in.

Making a mental note to either call or shoot a text right after the patient she was headed to see, Neysa knocked lightly on the door before entering, without permission being granted. Immediately noticing a beautiful chocolate little girl sitting patiently on the table with two long pig tails in her hair, she smiled; however, that smile quietly faded when she noticed the man in the room with her.

“Hello Dr. Brown. This my daughter Kayla, I’m Jayson Bishop. I don’t think we’ve been formally introduced.”

Neysa stood with her mouth wide open as Mr. Elevator extended his arm for a handshake. Taken back again by his looks, Neysa froze; she knew for a fact the last time she saw him would be the last time she saw him, but here he was, standing in front of her.

“Umm Ummmm…. Mr. Bishop, nice to meet you.” She spoke, quickly regaining her composure.

“And I take it that you are Princess Kayla.” Neysa turned to his baby girl and said, fixing the loose hairs in her ponytails.

“Yes.” She cheesed, shaking her head up and down.

“Daddy! She called me Princess like you!’ Kayla beamed, her big bright eyes lightening up the room.

“That’s cuz you are a Princess, like Dr. Brown here is a Queen.” Jay replied, his attention shifting from his daughter to Neysa.

An awkward silence captivated the room, this situation definitely being a first for Neysa.

“Sooooo, Princess, let me check you out. Stand up for me.” She finally spoke, helping Kayla onto the ground.

The routine check-up took less than ten minutes and Neysa was low-key sad that it was over. She loved Kayla; she was such a smart 8-year-old and well mannered, something that was rare nowadays. Kayla told Neysa about her birthday party, which a few months back, and how her dad was taking her to Disney's World. Listening to her stories warmed Neysa's heart and the entire time they talked, Jay remained quiet in the corner.

"Ok Princess, you can put your shoes back on while I talk to Daddy." Neysa told her before heading over to the computer.

"She's in perfect health. She's caught up on all her shots. We don't need to see her again for another six months." Neysa said, turning and smiling at Kayla before looking back at Jayson.

"But *I* need to see *you* before six months." He replied, biting his bottom lip as he walked closer to her, softly grabbing her hand.

Neysa's eyes slowly shifted from the computer's screen over to him, who stared into her eyes. No matter how much she tried to ignore the throbbing between her legs, she couldn't, that man was irresistible.

"I'm flattered Mr. Bishop, but I'm in a relationship and…."

"He ain't made you his wife." Jay cut her off and said, stepping in closer, the smell of Extra Peppermint gum on his breath.

"My number in my daughter's records. I hope to hear from you soon." Jay continued, bringing her hand up to his mouth, placing a soft kiss on her knuckles before grabbing his daughter and leaving out the room.

Standing there stuck, again, Neysa tried to figure out her next move when the phone inside the patient's room began to rang. Slightly startled, Neysa logged out of the system before answering the call.

"Dr. Brown." She spoke inside the receiver.

"Dr. Brown, your sister called, she said it's an emergency and to give her a call back ASAP!" Montana urgently reported.

"Okay. I'll call now." Neysa told her, going inside her pocket, noticing almost twenty missed calls mostly from Nicole, Dallas, and Ocean.

Seeing their names on the screen along with the message from Montana, Neysa nervously called her sister back first. The phone rung once before she heard Nicole's cries and screams.

"Nikki.... Nikki.... NICOLE! WHAT'S WRONG?" Neysa yelled into the phone, placing it on speaker before sitting down.

"It's Appa...It's Mommy.... I-I-"

"What's wrong with Daddy and Mommy, Nicole? What happened?" Neysa leg began to shake as she tried to get whatever it was out of her sister.

"They dead Neysa. They gone. MOMMY AND DADDY IS GONE!"

CHAPTER FIFTEEN

Dallas held Neysa's hand as they walked out the church doors towards the family car that waited for them at the curb. Her heart ached for her best friend, and although there was nothing she could do to make things better, she planned on being by her side through it all.

"Chinks already in the car. I'll be right behind you. Here come Ocean. See you at the cemetery." Dallas told her before placing a kiss on her cheek and walking away.

Looking both ways before she crossed the street, Dallas hurried to the car, so they could grab a good spot in the funeral line. With it almost being one-hundred degrees, she craved for cool air as for the church's air conditioner broke.

"She good? You ready?" Chinks asked the moment she entered the car.

Inhaling deeply, Dallas took a moment to appreciate the cool breeze before replying to her husband.

"Yeah, she's in the car. Ocean was walking up when I left. Let's go before everybody come out."

Chinks quickly maneuvered out of the parking lot, grabbing a spot only a few cars behind the black Jeeps Neysa and her family was in. Shaking her head from side to side, Dallas was in disbelief; she couldn't believe Mr. and Mrs. Sui was gone for real. They were like a second set of parents to Dallas, and although their relationship with Neysa was strained, they never treated her any differently.

"I can't believe this shit." Dallas said aloud to no one in particular as she pulled her shades down over her eyes.

"Yeah that was fuck'd up man." Chinks canted from behind the wheel, cracking the windows before lightning a blunt.

"Why not just take the money? Why they have to kill them too?" Dallas snarled, thinking about how the whole ordeal played out.

A week ago, one of Neysa's dad's nail shops was robbed, but instead of simply taking the money, they shot both Mr. and Mrs. Sui in the head.

"These stupid ass niggas these days ain't got shit to lose but everything to prove." Chinks replied, inhaling and exhaling deeply, a thick cloud of smoke escaping his nostrils.

"That's the fucked-up part!" Dallas yelled, banging her fist on the costumed -made orange leather dashboard inside his car.

“My bad.” She laughed, noticing the look on his face before continuing.

“I gotta ask you a question and I need you to be honest with me.” Dallas paused, waiting on a response from him.

“What’s up?” Chinks said, looking at her out the side of his eyes.

“No promise.”

“Go ahead Dallas. I promise.” He nonchalantly assured her, just as the funeral line began to move.

“Ok so look right. You know I’m NEVVEEERRRR in yo street business and…”

“DALLAS! ASK THE FUCKN’ QUESTION!” He barked, banging his hands on the sterling wheel.

“Damn, my bad nigga, but ok…. you soooooooooo impatient.” She held her invisible pearls and retorted.

“Since what happened to Neysa’s parents took place in one of y’all hood, I was wondering if Ocean was gone handle that?” Dallas finally got out, sitting up straight in the leather seats.

"On some real shit, he ain't said shit to me about it." Chinks informed her, switching lanes with the line of cars.

"Okay so then can I ask for a favor?" she asked, looking over at him as he did the same.

"What up baby?"

"Can you handle it for me? You know Neysa means the world to me, and I just feel like their family will sleep better at night knowing that …."

"Say less baby. It's done." Chinks cut her off mid-sentence and finalized, silencing her the rest of the ride.

The burial went smoother than she had expected and as promised, Dallas held Neysa's hand the entire time. Although she was taking her parents death well on the outside, D knew her bestie far too well and it was all for show.

"Bae, can you grab my flip flops out the back?" Dallas said to Chinks before getting out of the car and heading inside the repast.

Unbuckling the straps on her Giuseppe heels, Dallas grabbed the pink Old Navy flip flops from her husband and put them on. Her feet were killing her, and she refused to suffer any longer.

"You so fuckn' beautiful man." Chinks complimented her with a smile as he held the front door open for her.

Grinning and winking her right eyes, Dallas skated past but waited for him to catch up before they locked hands and entered the hall.

"There go Ocean over there. "Chinks announced, pointing to his homie who sat off in the corner alone.

"Aight. I see Shonnie and Trinity over there. I'll catch up to you later baby." Dallas replied before the two met in the middle for a kiss.

Going their separate ways, Dallas spoke to a few familiar faces before arriving at the table with her girls. Both Shonnie and Trinity looked beautiful in their lavender and white, the requested colors by Neysa and Nicole.

"Hey beauties!" Dallas greeted them, the both of them standing, embracing her with a hug.

"Y'all seen Neysa?" Dallas asked, taking a seat in the chair across from Trinity.

"Last time I seen her, she was taking her nephew to the restroom but that was about five minutes ago." Shonnie noted as Dallas's eyes searched the crowd for her.

"Oooop! There she go right there. I'll be back." She announced, removing herself from the table.

Gliding through the crowd once again, Dallas kept her eyes on Neysa, careful not to lose sight of her. The place was getting packed, and with everyone wearing the same colors, they all blended.

"Aye...Aye…Aye heifer, hold up!" Dallas tugged at the tail of Neysa's blouse just as she began to wonder off.

"I been looking for you. You good?" she continued once Neysa turned around.

"I been looking for yo ass. I'm straight. Just need to get high. Where Ocean?"

Before Dallas could respond, Neysa must've spotted the guys at the table because that's the direction she headed in. Following close behind her, Dallas laughed as Neysa did her best to avoid conversation with certain guests. She wasn't trying to be rude; she needed a blunt and if you knew Neysa, you knew why.

"Who got some weed?" Dallas stepped up and asked first, turning all heads in her direction.

"Depends on who asking." Chinks replied, giving her the side eye.

"I am." Dallas proudly stated with her head held high.

"You don't even smoke. Gon' somewhere." Ocean chimed in, dismissing her and handing an already rolled blunt to Neysa.

After being dragged outside, Dallas and Neysa walked down the street while she smoked her weed. The strong scent, and even stronger wind, smacked her in the face, giving her that first "high off contact" moment. She could tell by the silence and look in Neysa's eyes that she was enjoying it too.

"Aye Dallas. I got a question." Neysa said out of the blue, just as they turned the corner.

"Yeah, what's up?" She replied, slightly eager to hear what she had to say, especially since she had yet to open up after the double murders.

"You seen Trinity's face? Don't it look like somebody beat her ass?" Neysa blurted out, causing Dallas to stop dead in her tracks.

"NO BITCH! WHAT!" she yelled out, thinking back now to the time she spent at the table with them.

"Come on, I'm for real. It looks like Shonnie did her best to beat the shit outta her face, but I can still see marks around her neck." Neysa explained as the wheels in Dallas's brain began to spin.

"Nope. Imma be honest. I ain't even look at her like that."

"GIRL, SINCE WHEN?" Neysa smacked her lips and yelled out dramatically.

Stopping again, Dallas bent over laughing at how extra she was being. She was happy to see that she was in great spirits, even if that meant she was the butt of her jokes.

"I ain't mean it like that, you asshole. I was saying, I wasn't at the table long enough to notice, but now, I wanna know." Dallas told her just as they turned around, heading back to the hall."

It was the truth, she hadn't noticed, and on top of that, Dallas was no longer attracted to Trinity in that light anyway. Yes, she was still a bad bitch, but Dallas preferred a friendship over anything else. In addition, with them starting a family, that freaky shit had to come to an end.

CHAPTER SIXTEEN

2 Months Later

"HE WHAT?" Shonnie yelled into the phone so loud, Trinity had to pull it back from her ear.

"He raped me." She whispered shamefully before tears poured from her eyes.

"CALL THE FUCKN' POLICE NOW!" Shonnie screamed. Trinity could tell that she was moving about in the background.

"Is that why you've been distant? It's been weeks and this the most conversation I've gotten out of you. Trinity, you could have told me." She continued as Trini flopped down on the bed.

"I know friend, I'm sorry, but you have to understand, that shit fuck'd me up. I took a leave from work. The only person I've spoken to was Aunt Shelia and that's because she doesn't take no for an answer." Trinity explained before standing to her feet and heading into the bathroom to take a Tylenol.

As of lately, she's been getting these unexplainable headaches but finally that morning, she made an appointment to check things out. She had been hiding from the world since the incident happened with Rico. After being choked out and practically tortured for hours, when he did finally leave, he never returned.

Trinity called the cops, changed the locks, and made plans to sue the building her condo was in. There was no way in the world with the amount she was paying for rent, she should be that accessible, especially to an insane person like Rico.

"Look, I'm on my way over there. I'll grab some wine. We'll finish this conversation when I get there." Shonnie assured her before ending the call.

Turning on the shower, Trinity adjusted the water to her liking before jumping in. Washing her body over twice, she rinsed off before grabbing a dry towel and making her exit. Forgetting the windows were up, the cool October air breezed across her body, forming goosebumps and hardening her nipples. Grabbing a pair of boy shorts and an oversized shirt, Trinity placed her hair in a high ponytail and headed to the kitchen. Going inside the refrigerator, she grabbed a couple pieces of fruit, along with a knife and chopping board. Cleaning off the merchandise, Trinity then cut them into small pieces before placing them neatly on a tray.

Rushing over to her ringing phone, Trinity snatched it open, placing it on speaker.

"So, look right. I ran into Dallas and Neysa at the liquor store. They wanna come over, but I know you not in the mood so…."

"Bring 'em, I need to be around love tonight." Trinity cut her off and stated, figuring a girl's night is exactly what she needed.

Fixing up the place and preparing more snacks, Trinity was lighting candles and getting settled by the time her girls arrived. Greeting them at the door, they all dished out huge hugs before getting acquainted in the living room.

"Ummmmm Trinity, where the fuck you been? I haven't seen you since the funeral." Neysa said, taking a bite from the strawberry that hung from her wine glass.

"I been dealing with some shit y'all and I apologize." She replied, looking down into her lap.

"No need for apologies, we adults, we all tend to go through some shit. Just know that you not alone anymore. You got us bitch." Dallas exclaimed, her words truly touching Trinity's heart.

As it is known, Trinity made it through life pretty much on her own. With no siblings, or even parents, she had friends but was never part of a close circle. Having Shonnie and now Dallas and Neysa in corner, Trinity felt more confident about opening up and letting people in.

"When I was in Atlanta, I dated a clown name Rico. Long story short, I fell in love with the devil. He started beating my ass and controlling my life. Of course, he was into the drug game and like most niggas, he got popped. Got sentenced to some time and during that time, I moved on. I told Rico over and over again that it wasn't working, but he wasn't trying to hear it. I cut off all communication, praying that he got the picture, but he never did. When I got word that he was being released, I moved back here, thinking I was off the radar. Fast forward two months ago, he found me. Popped up, beat my ass, and…. and he raped me."

By the time Trinity was done, all four women was in tears, wrapping their arms around her. Their love and embrace seeped through, causing her to cry even harder. The feeling she got was overwhelming, and she knew she made the right decision by letting them in. After answering all of their questions and listening to the advice they distributed, Trinity felt so much better knowing that they had her back.

“So, has he contacted you since then?” Dallas turned to her and asked just as they cracked open another bottle of Stella Rosa.

“I blocked him on EVERYTHING but that don’t mean shit for him.”

“How about you come stay with me until you find another place? You know I got an extra room, and it won’t be of any inconvenience.” Shonnie told her but Trinity shook her head no.

“I’m tired of running from that nigga. Imma move but on my own time. Fuck him.” She hissed, tossing the glass back, emptying it.

Vibing until almost two in the morning, the girls finally decided to part ways. Feeling the effects from the wine and hookah, Trinity locked up after they left and headed to the bedroom when her phone rung. Pressing ignore and rolling her eyes to the back of head, she tossed it on the bed before heading to use washroom. Once she was done, she washed her hands and returned back to the room but not before stopping at the full-length mirror in her walk-in closet. Smiling at the sight before her, not only did she look good, she was glowing. Lifting her shirt, she took her hands and rubbed it over her protruding belly and laughed devilishly.

"Thanks RICO!"

CHAPTER SEVENTEEN

Neysa placed the yellow tulips near her parents' headstone and wiped her eyes before turning to walk away. It had almost been three months since their killings and with each day, it haunted her more. Guilt filled her conscious as she thought back to the last moments she had with them. No, they didn't have the perfect relationship, but Neysa knew they always wanted best for her. And for that, she'll forever be grateful.

"Dallas, let me call you back. I'm leaving the cemetery, and I gotta let Ocean know that I'm on my way."

Ending the call, Neysa did as she said and call Ocean, only for the voicemail to pick up.

"This nigga bet not be sleep." She said aloud as she started her car, preparing to head home.

Just as she was about to call him back, an incoming call came in from him, saving his life.

"I'm on my way. You dressed?" Neysa asked before placing the call on speaker and turning into traffic.

"Damn baby, I'm not gon' be able to make it. I gotta handle some business and ----"

"I don't wanna hear that shit Ocean. You knew about Maggie's birthday party months ago, and you promised that you were going to go."

Hearing Ocean's excuses as to why he was going back on his word, yet again, drove Neysa insane. Since the death of her parents, he had become more unavailable, and she couldn't pinpoint why. Of course, Ocean blamed it on working but something inside of her knew that was bullshit too.

"Look, how about we grab Maggie one weekend and take her ----"

"Fuck you…BYE!" Neysa spat, ending the call while he was in mid-sentence.

Calling back twice and sending a text, Neysa ignored him and headed to her Goddaughter's party, alone. Pissed, she searched for something to listen to while she drove but came up short. Grabbing her phone, she called Dallas back, maybe she had something to say that'll brighten up her day.

"BITTTCCCCHHHHH…. TELL ME WHY TRINITY PREGNANT!" Dallas yelled into the phone before Neysa knew it had connected.

"Pregnant? Girl, what?"

"Yes, so remember she told us about buddy breaking in and raping her? Well, according to Shonnie, he got her ass pregnant too." Dallas told her without stopping to take a breath.

"Swear to God. What she gon' do about the baby? I meannnnn…."

"Well ok, listen up. Remember the tattoo I gave her? Those numbers were the date she had a stillborn. Shonnie said Trinity has a tough time conceiving as well and so…."

"SHE KEEPING THE BABY BY THE CRAZY RAPIST?" Neysa screamed as Dallas laughed on the other end.

"YUP! But in her defense, I can see why. Yeah, the nigga crazy, but she don't need his ass to be a mother, especially when being a mother means so much to her. It's not like he a stranger who took the shit and got her popped off… she was in a whole relationship with this nigga."

Dallas's words actually made sense to Neysa, although there's no chance in hell she'll do it.

"Well, she's a better woman than me cuz bay-beeee…. Planned Parenthood, here I come!"

Neysa and Dallas chatted a little more about Trinity's situation and how they were going to be there for her as if she was one of them. Dallas shared with her the decision she made regarding starting her own family. Neysa knew the struggles her best friend dealt with, having fertility issues. Her and Chinks had been trying to conceive since they were teenagers. It wasn't until they became older when she started caring. Having a career, husband, and millions in the bank was ideal and now was the time to expand.

"What time you say Maggie's party started and Ocean gon' meet you there?" Dallas recalled, bringing Neysa's attitude right back.

"He not going, he backed out once again, but I'm headed there now!"

"I'm not gon' even ask why, but you know what you SHOULD do!" Dallas's voice peaked like she came up with the plan of the century.

Scared to ask what, Neysa remained quiet until she started back up.

"Call that nigga you met TWICE at work and tell that nigga to meet you there. You say he got a kid, right?

GURL, fuck Ocean, for right now cuz he still my bro, and let someone else put a smile on your face for once."

"Nah man, I don't wanna lead nobody on and having them think I'm interested when…."

"When you ARE, Neysa. Bitch, you stole the man's number from his child's medical records." Dallas cut her off and said, just before they both erupted in laughter.

"BITCH! It was a bet. You bet me to do it."

"We ain't twelve, you a grown ass woman, you took his number because YOU WANTED HIS NUMBER."

Whether Neysa wanted to admit it or not, Dallas was right. The physical attraction was there the moment she stepped foot on that elevator and the fact they he somehow, someway, got an appointment to see her, turned Neysa on even more.

"Aight fuck. Imma call you back."

Building up enough courage along with being vulnerable as fuck, Neysa went into her address book to dial Jayson's number, getting an answer on the third ring.

"YOOOO DOC!" his deep voiced rang through the speakers in her car, putting a huge smile on her face.

"How the fuck you know it was me?" She beamed, turning the volume knob up a few notches.

Hearing him chuckle lightly caused goosebumps to form on her skin. Cracking the window slightly, Neysa switched lanes, preparing for her exit.

"The phone said, *"N. Brown"* baby, you gotta give me a reason to stalk first." Jay spoke, making Neysa completely forget about caller ID.

"Oh, my bad." She embarrassedly blushed through the phone.

"But I was calling to invite you and Kayla to my Goddaughter's party. It's today and super last minute but…."

"Drop the addy and we'll meet you there."

Slightly taken back, Neysa ended the call and did as she was told. Jay texted back letting her know he was in the area and should be arriving around the same time as her. Now in the mood to hear some music, Neysa turned to Beyoncé's station on Pandora and grooved the rest of the way. Pulling along the curb across the street from the Miller's home, Neysa killed the engine before checking her reflection in the sun visor. Pleased at the sight before her, she prepared to get out when her phone chimed.

773-893-9389: This me parking behind you.

Smiling at the phone, Neysa pulled it from the charger and got out without responding. Adjusting the leather jacket she wore, she pulled the Fashion Nova jeans over her ass and stepped off the curb.

"Damn ma, them hospital scrubs don't do you no justice." Jay stated with a smirk the moment his wheat Timbs hit the concrete.

Flattered and unable to hide her rosy cheeks, Neysa thanked him with a smile before waiting on him to join, heading over towards his car.

"Hey Princess. Nice to see you again."

Jay's daughter Kayla was just as beautiful as she remembered. Dressed in a cream Gucci sweater dress, a pair of red knitted stockings, and colorful JoJo Siwa sneakers, Neysa admired her attire and knew her father was to blame.

"I told her that shit ain't match." Neysa heard Jay say from behind her as if he was reading her mind.

Turning around and laughing at him, Neysa grabbed Kayla's hand, assisting her across the street towards Maggie's house.

"I can't wait for you to meet my Goddaughter Maggie. I think you two will have so much fun together." Neysa looked down at the top of Kayla's pigtails and stated as she eagerly jumped around.

"Let's go through the side doors. The party in the basement." She then turned to tell Jay who walked a few feet behind them.

Dressed in the same style Gucci sweater as his daughter and a pair of destressed jeans, Neysa couldn't deny the attraction she had for him. The nigga was knocking on perfect in her eyes, making her regret her decision to call him. Following the party décor to the door, Neysa rang the bell before entering the marble and stainless-steel kitchen.

"Godddddd---Mommmmmyyyyy!" Maggie's loud yet squeaky voice and petite frame came from running out of the kitchen and into Neysa's arms.

Hugging her tight and lifting her off the ground, Neysa swung her around before placing her back on her feet. She missed Maggie so much, and although they stayed in fair distance, she didn't see her often.

"Let me introduce you to my new friend, her name is Kayla. This is Kayla's dad, Jay. Y'all, this my baby

Maggie." Neysa bubbly introduced the gang to each other before they headed in the basement.

Doing the same introduction with Mr. and Mrs. Miller, Kayla left them, joining the other kids in fun games and activities. After making sure that they weren't hungry, Jay asked Neysa to step outside with him and she happily accepted.

"Wanna sit in the car or you cool out here?" he asked her, just as they made it out front.

The weather was beautiful that October day, and although she wanted to feel the breeze, thoughts of Ocean popping up scared the fuck out of her. He had been calling and texting because he knew he was wrong, but Neysa played the mad role and didn't answer.

"We can sit in yo car." She finally replied, stepping towards the street as he hit the locks on his midnight blue Porsche Cheyanne.

Stepping into the truck, Neysa admired the customized interior, specifically the colors inside the dashboard. She couldn't believe she was inside another man's ride, knowing how crazy her man was. In the past, Neysa went on dates during the times they were separated, but what she was doing with Jay was different. She was actually starting to like him.

CHAPTER EIGHTEEN

"But what you mean, maybe we should wait? Where the fuck did this come from? Wait for what nigga? I'm your wife! What the fuck is you saying?"

Dallas's mouth went fifty miles per hour as she fussed and cussed at Chinks. The audacity of him, she couldn't believe he had the nerve to tell her to wait.

"Listen Dallas, I'm not saying that I don't want to start a family. You know I'm not saying that shit. This has been a goal of ours since forever. All I'm saying is, I wanna get out the game fully before we do so. Having kids a big deal, and I can't live happily with you or my babies looking over their shoulders every ten minutes." Chinks yelled from the bathroom, the shower water running in the background.

She had finally built up enough courage to tell him about Dr. Turner and how she was their lord and savior. After test and test, things were starting to look up for her fertility treatment. Being disappointment so much in the past, Dallas decided to surprise Chinks once she knew Dr. Turner was the one. Imagine the look on her face now, knowing that he feels they should wait.

"Okay, so get out the shit NOW! This don't mean I'm going to be pregnant tomorrow, and it takes damn near a year to carry a child. Nigga, you have time to get the fuck out." She screamed, noticing his phone lightening up on the nightstand.

Standing to her feet, Dallas walked over and picked it up, noticing a few unread messages on the screen. Entering the password, Dallas waited for the phone to unlock, but it never happened.

"Wrong passcode. The fuck." She cursed under her breath as she put the numbers in again.

"Why the fuck he changed the code?" Dallas asked herself before yelling it out loud.

"WHY THE FUCK YOU CHANGE YO CODE?" She screamed into the bathroom, just as Chinks appeared at the door with a beige towel wrapped around his waist.

"Why you going through my shit?" he snapped, snatching the phone out of her hands.

Quickly jumping to her feet, Dallas stepped to Chinks, standing on her tip toes so they could be eye level. He had her fucked up, snatching anything out of her hands like she was a kid.

"Since when we keeping secrets and shit?"

"Secrets? How the fuck I'm keeping secrets? Move out my way before I miss my flight Dallas."

"Fuck yo flight, Marquis. Fuck you. Fuck yo flight. And fuck that dusty ass phone and password." She snapped, meaning each and every word.

It never failed, it seemed as if they always got into a huge argument right before he took a business trip. With distribution centers in various states, Chinks was often away from home and Dallas didn't mind until recently. She blamed it on getting older and simply wanting more; it was too bad her husband didn't with stain the same mentality.

"Look baby. When I get back, we'll sit down and look further into our future. I love you and I want nothing more than to put 'bout six in you and I promise that's going to happen." Chinks grabbed her by the shoulders and assured her, placing soft kisses on her neck.

Rolling her eyes to the back of her head, Dallas broke loose from his grip, grabbed her phone and keys. and walked away. Another one of Chinks long-time moves, fuck her brains out, that way she'll forget she was mad by the time he gets back. Dallas knew the man like the back of her hand; therefore, she knew how to navigate when dealing with him.

"So, you ain't gon' drop me off at the airport?" Chinks yelled out to Dallas's back as she headed down the stairs and out the door.

"YOU BETTER UBER NIGGA. SAFE FLIGHT!" She screamed back before slamming the door shut and stepping onto the porch.

Zipping up her cream Canada Goose jacket, Dallas hurried to the car, looking back occasionally to see if Chinks appeared. With no sign of him, she cranked up the engine and headed towards her first destination, *Can't Believe It's Not Meat.* Since being on this new health kick, Dallas decided to look into more options, starting with a new place her clients have been raving about. On top of trying new things, she was meeting her girls there, and with the day she had, she needed to vent to them.

"Nice to see that everyone can tell time.... DALLAS!" Neysa started up the moment she arrived at the table.

Giving her the finger, she hugged both Shonnie and Trinity before taking a seat and grabbing the menu.

"I already know what I want, they got this Oreo milkshake and it's fye!" Trinity exclaimed excitedly like a kid.

"Slow down big momma!" Shonnie chimed in, causing all the girls to laugh.

"Wait. That's right. You are eating for two now." Neysa threw in, causing Dallas to laugh to herself.

Neysa wasn't being shady, however, the bitch was being nosey. Since Shonnie spilled the beans, the girls hadn't spent any time together, but with Neysa asking the questions, they were sure to make up for lost time.

"Okay, so how far along are you? Who's your doctor? You been taking prenatal pills? Do that crazy bastard know? I commend you for being strong during a time like this cause Lord knows if it was me, I ----"

"NEYSA! CHILL! DAMN!" Dallas blurted out, interrupting her best friend's rant and making them all giggle.

"Well I'm sorry, that the PEDIATRICIAN in me, cares…. BITCH!" Neysa cursed at her, just as they prepared to place their orders.

Once that was done and out the way, the ladies tuned in as Trinity broke everything down, even answering all of Neysa's questions.

"I haven't heard from him since it happened but that means nothing for Rico. I know y'all might think I'm crazy for keeping a man's baby that raped me, but it's deeper than that. Trust. I'm eleven weeks, and I go for another ultrasound in another two weeks. My aunt is so excited… of course I didn't tell her the whole story, she'll lose her mind if she knew what really happened. I'm moving next month to a bigger place, and I plan on getting some type of order against Rico…."

Trinity rambled on through their meal while the three women listened attentively, giving all sound advice to their friend. Sitting there with mixed emotions, Dallas was happy for Trinity but secretly envious; she too wanted to experience pregnancy. Learning of Trinity's fertility issues, which was similar to hers, Dallas however felt a sense of hope, which was something she desperately needed.

"Ok, so I was thinking… Let's do a small gender reveal. Nothing ghetto and hood like the clips you see on Facebook but something simple and elegant." Dallas spoke, changing not only the mood for her but for the table as well.

"I'm with it!" Shonnie geeked as Neysa threw out random ideas.

"No. No. No. No y'all. I'm too old for that shit. I'll find out when I find out." Trinity protested from her chair as she shook her head from side to side.

"Bullshit. Ain't nun of us got kids, and we love you so we gon' roll with Dallas's idea." Shonnie told her, shutting her up as they began to plan.

As the wheels turned in their heads, Dallas's phone rung, an incoming call from her shop manager, Zarkia.

"Hey boo, y'all good?" Dallas answered, hearing what sounded like a bunch of arguing in the background.

"Everything good. We got Flava of Love on the big screens, that's them hoes on tv… BUTTTTTTT I am calling for a reason." Zarkia paused as Dallas waited to hear what was next.

"A guy came in today and requested you."

"What guy?"

"I've never heard of him, but he did leave his card. I told him that you're normally unavailable, but he insisted, even left a check for two-thousand dollars to insure a spot."

Hearing the amount of money sparked her interest, only big shots left that type of deposit and according to Kia, he wasn't known.

“Well, I can tell he’s not from here, just by his accent and the number on his card is an Atlanta area code. I told him that I’ll get back to him.” Zarkia continued as they wrapped things up at the table.

“Call him and tell him I’ll do it, but make sure he knows the rules as far as time slots and deposits are concerned. I’m about to swing by there now. Y’all ate?” Dallas asked.

“Yeah, we grabbed Hooters and that shipment of ink came in this morning. You gon’ love that shit!” she beamed through the phone; Dallas smiling at her enthusiasm.

“Aight. I’ll see you in a minute.”

“Wait Kia, what did you say homie name was?” Dallas quizzed, catching her before the call ended.

“Ummmm hold on, let me grab the card…. Ummmm, his name is…. Antonio.”

CHAPTER NINETEEN

Hearing her baby's heartbeat warmed Trinity's heart like no other. After the loss of her daughter last year, Trinity's mind hadn't been the same since then. Struggling to get pregnant, she carried a baby full term, only to lose her on the delivery table. Dealing with all of this alone, she was scared and afraid to go through it again, but something about this time seemed different.

"You're all set, see you in a month." The Medical Assistant said to her with a smile before handing her a card with the next appointment listed.

Heading to her car, Trinity decided to place an order with Wing Stop before going back to the office. Grabbing her food and a big gulp from 7-Eleven, Trinity drove through downtown Chicago, admiring the beautiful skyline. Preparing to turn inside the parking garage, Trinity whole body jerked when a car came out of nowhere and side swiped her car, leaving the side mirror hanging for dear life.

"WHAT THE FUCK!" She screamed out in frustration as the car sped away, leaving her with only a glimpse, a glimpse that she wishes she hadn't gotten.

Shook up and afraid, Trinity quickly parked in her spot, killed the engine, grabbed her food, and exited the car. Making sure to check her surroundings, she headed inside her building in a hurry.

"Ms. Howard, how was your appointment?" Susie, the front desk receptionist, asked as soon as the glass doors opened.

"It was fantastic, thanks for asking." She replied with a fake smile as she stormed past her into her office.

Flicking on the lights, Trinity closed the door shut and proceeded to her desk when she noticed a bouquet of red flowers waiting for her. Slowly walking over, Trinity's eyes surveilled the small room as if she was searching for clues. Usually, Susie told her whenever any delivers came, maybe it slipped her mind.

"Hey Susie, who sat these roses on my desk?" Trinity reopened the door and asked, sticking her head out to get a clear view.

"Ah, Ms. Howard, I have no clue. I've been here since you left, and no one has gotten passed me." She replied before Trinity closed the door again with no response.

Snatching the note from the roses, Trinity took a moment to smell them before reading over the contents on the card.

I remember how much you love these, they're your favorite.

I peeped you going to the clinic.

I hope all is well....

If not, let these cheer you up.

~Rico

Just as she expected, he was back, and Trinity was more so pissed than she was afraid. She knew he wasn't going away that easily; she just had no clue as to how soon he would return. Rushing over to the other side of her desk, Trinity pulled off her leather jacket before taking a seat. Entering the password into her MacBook Pro, Trinity froze, taking a mental break before proceeding. Grabbing her phone, she scrolled through her log, stopping on an unsaved number. Her right leg shaking under her desk, Trinity waited for an answer, only to get the voicemail again. She hated being ignored, or at least feeling like she was, and that's exactly how she felt at that moment. Vibrating in her hand, a message came through from the number, causing her to smack her lips.

"Can't answer but can text." She fused aloud to herself as she opened and read the text message.

312-893-0089: I'm busy right now bae, you good?

Rolling her eyes to the back of her head, she used both hands to text back quicker, making sure to leave nothing out.

Trinity: Of course but this is a 911 situation.... Rico back and although I told you NOT to get involved.... I NEED you to get involved now. The nigga hit my car when I was coming from the clinic. IDGAF if you gotta kill that nigga in CHICAGO OR ATLANTA.... just make sure he's dead!!!

312-893-0089: DONE!

Placing the phone screen-down on the cherry oakwood desk, Trinity went to her laptop, where she pulled up a few files. After searching for almost ten minutes, she finally found what she was looking for. Making sure she dotted all her "I's" and crossed all her "T's," Trinity picked up her office phone to call in a favor.

"Ms. Howard, didn't expect I'll see your number. What do I owe the pleasure?" Steve's smooth voice spoke through the receiver and into her ear.

A slight grin parted her full lips before she shook her head from side to side. Something about her former boss drove her up a wall, whether that be a good or bad thing. He was a high-status lawyer who knew people in high places, especially in the legal world.

"I need a favor." She blurted out, getting right to the point.

"And I need a date, maybe more depending on YOUR favor."

Rolling her eyes deep in the back of her head, Trinity let out a long sigh before agreeing to his demands. She knew that even if Steve thought he was going to fuck, he had another thing coming. Giving him the run down, Steve assured Trinity that it was an easy task and that he was one call away whenever she was ready to make things shake. Using him only as a backup in case Plan A didn't work, she refused to allow Rico to threaten the health of her child.

CHAPTER TWENTY

"Ocean… stopppppp! I gotta go. Dallas should be pulling up any minute now." Neysa whined as she squirmed out of his muscular arms.

What was supposed to be a quickie turned out to be three rounds, and now she was rushing to get dressed.

"The engagement party starts in an hour, and we still have to pick up Shonnie and Trinity." She continued to explain as she placed a gold hoop earring in her ear.

"Aye. Who getting married again?" Ocean asked as he pulled up a pair of Calvin Klein boxer briefs.

"Sequaya, Chinks' cousin. It's a surprise and we gotta get there before she does."

Sliding into a black fitted body con dress, Neysa fixed the diamond cut neckless that rested on her neck before sliding into a pair of black Christian Louboutin pumps.

"Speaking of surprises, I got one for you before you leave." Ocean walked over to her slowly and stated, rubbing lotion into both hands.

"Nah big fella. I'm good on YO type of surprises. I told you I gotta go." She held up both hands and replied, backing away from him.

Laughing, displaying those perfect white teeth that she loved so much, Ocean stopped in his tracks and stared at her.

"What?" Neysa twisted her head to the side and asked as she adjusted Pandora bracelet on her wrist.

"You so beautiful baby." He declared, staring directly into her brown eyes.

"Thank you." She blushed.

"But what's the surprise?"

"I handled that issue regarding your parents, and although it'll never bring them back, I wanted you and Nicole to sleep better at night knowing those muthafuckers not breathing."

Without having to ask any further questions, Neysa fell into Oceans arms and began to cry. It was one of the few times she actually cried, but it felt good. There had been no major leads and Neysa was starting to feel like it was a closed case. Ocean was right, revenge wouldn't bring them back, but it felt good knowing them bitches weren't breathing either.

"Look man. Fix yo face, Dallas out there blowing like she lost her muthafucking mind. Have a good time tonight. I love you. See you later." Ocean held her chin and said as she wiped the tears away.

Spraying on her favorite perfume, Neysa kissed Ocean, grabbed her clutch, and headed out the door to her impatient best friend. After complimenting each other on their fabulous looks, Dallas drove in the direction of Shonnie's house, so they could get their night started.

"So, what's been up? How you and the new boo?" Dallas cut the music down and asked, grinning from ear to ear.

"He's not my boo. We just friends annnndddddd, we good. We text all day. I'm facetiming him when I'm not around Ocean. I mean, he cool.... I guess."

"BITCH PLEASE! I GUESS MY ASS! YOU LIKE THAT MAN.... LET ME SEE A PICTURE." Dallas screamed as if they were not sitting next to each other.

"I don't have a picture." She lied.

"And besides, Imma have to cut it off with him cause I'm starting to feel bad. Me and Ocean been in a good space lately, and I don't wanna fuck that up. I believe in karma, and I'll hate to lead Jay on, and that shit comes back on me." She truthfully stated this time.

"You right friend. You know yo heart, and if you feel that leaving that good ass nigga alone is the right then to do, then I'm with it too." Dallas replied while Neysa wondered was she being sarcastic or not.

With traffic being backed up due to a concert at the United Center, Dallas did her best to take short cuts, finally arriving at Shonnie's place forty minutes later.

"So, I wanted to ask you something before they got in the car. You think Trinity stupid for keeping this nigga's baby?" Dallas said as she blew the horn for the ladies to come out.

"Ehhhhh.... You know what Imma say. But why? Why you ask?"

"Just asking."

"You a just asking lie. Why?" Neysa asked her again, pulling down the sun visor, checking her makeup in the mirror.

"JUST ASKING. Now shut up. Here they come."

Neysa watched as Shonnie and Trinity made their way to the car. Noticing how much Trinity's belly had grown, Neysa made a mental note to mention it to Dallas later just before they got in. Once the greetings were out of the way, the four of them danced to Megan Thee Stallion without a care in the world. Pulling in front of what seemed to be a banquet hall, Dallas killed the engine as everyone got out so valet could get in. Having only met Chinks' cousin Sequaya a few times, Neysa could tell the type of lifestyle they lived from the fancy spot.

"I hope the soon to be bride not here yet, and we haven't missed the reveal." Trinity said as they entered the doors, leading them into a dining room area.

Upon entering, Neysa noticed two long tables full of people, sitting in front of empty plates as if they were waiting to be served. The closer she walked in, the more she recognized every single face and that's when the tears began to flow. The room was full of family and friends belonging to both her and Ocean. Standing on a stage, wearing a black and maroon tuxedo, Ocean held a microphone in his hand while everyone in the place stared at her and smiled. With phones in their hands, everyone recorded what turned out to truly be a surprise.

"Ummmm Ocean baby, what's going on?" she mouthed to him as he stood there smiling, waiting for her to approach.

Grabbing his hand, Ocean assisted Neysa onto the small stage where he turned to face her before speaking.

"We been through so much shit, and the same way I've hurt you in the past, in front of these same people, I felt it was only right to have that same energy and confess my love in front of these same faces as well. Almost fifteen years in it, it's time I stopped playing and make you my wife." Ocean paused, leaving not one dry tear in the room.

"You gon' be my wife, Neysa? You gon' marry me?" Ocean got down on one knee and asked.

Unable to speak, Neysa shook her head up and down as she tried to control the tears. Once her answer was official, everyone in the room stood to their feet and cheered, congratulating the new couple.

"Let me see the ring. Let me see the ring." Shonnie eagerly said once Neysa reunited with the crew.

Showing off the 6-carat emerald cut diamond ring to her friends, Neysa felt like she was floating on cloud nine. This was so unexpected, which made her wonder how he pulled it off.

"And heffa, you ain't told me nothing." Neysa fussed, swinging her clutch bag in Dallas's direction.

"Bitch, ain't nobody told me shit. You see these tears? I'm just as shocked as you." She replied wiping her eyes, clearly still filled with excitement.

It was true, Ocean purposely didn't include Dallas in on the plans because she couldn't hold water. Chinks knew, along with Shonnie, but everyone had to swear not to tell Neysa or Dallas. Realizing that he had a point and good reasoning, Neysa knew too that telling her best friend would have been a bad idea.

With an open bar, a dope DJ, and rental hours until two in the morning, Neysa and the people she loved most in the world enjoyed their night. Neysa couldn't remember a time before when she was happier; it was literally the best night of her life.

CHAPTER TWENTY-ONE

Dallas walked through Queenz Tatt laughing as her all female crew of tattoo artist participated in a friendly twerk contest. "She Got A Dunk" by Souljah Boy blasted through the empty shop, just before opening time. Loving what she built, Dallas looked around, smiling in amazement at her biggest accomplishment.

"Don't forget you got that four o'clock. I texted him and he confirmed this morning, so you all set. Robin is booked, per usual. Shona running late, but she's pretty much booked too. Miko taking all walk-ins annnnndddddd someone needs to cover for me at seven, I'm doing a piercing."

Notating mentally everything Zarkia was saying, Dallas continued her strut to the office with attempts to finish paperwork before her client arrived. The end of the year was approaching, and she needed to gather all her tax documents and calculate her expenses. Closing the door shut behind her, Dallas went over and took a seat in the black leather chair behind her desk. Grabbing her cell phone, she went directly to Facebook and started scrolling through her feed. Stopping on a photo of Neysa and Ocean with her displaying her ring. Dallas shared the picture with cute emojis before closing the app and facetiming her newly engaged best friend.

"Ms. Brown or should I say Mrs. Carter?" Dallas said into the phone, the moment Neysa picked up.

"Say…. Heyyyy Mrs. Carter!" she replied in her best Beyoncé impersonation, sending Dallas into a laughing frenzy.

"What's the tea, girl? How you feeling?" D finally asked once she was able to speak.

"I'm good, girl. Waiting on Ocean to get back from the store. What you got going on?" Neysa quizzed from the other end of the phone.

"Shit. Got that appointment with dude in about twenty minutes." She paused, looking down at the Rolex on her arm.

"And speaking of dude, have to talked to Jay?" Dallas continued as she rambled through a stack of gold manila folders.

"Girrllllll…. So, I texted him and told him we needed to talk. I wanted to do the shit over the phone, but for some reason he refused, so we meeting up tonight."

Dallas listened as Neysa talked more about her life and the many things going on in it. She was truly happy that she was happy, and although she didn't see it coming, she was glad that it did.

"Ok best friend, somebody at the door, I'll call you later."

"Come in." Dallas yelled out before ending the call with Neysa.

"Chillllleeee. Yo four o'clock here.... With his fine ass!" Kia lustfully announced as Dallas stood to her feet, stepping from around the desk.

"He's at your station waiting.... and while you at it, can you see if he's single and like women? I mean, I'll even do step kids for him, just for *him* though.' She rambled on while Dallas laughed at her silliness.

Leaving out the office with Zarkia in tow, Dallas walked through the maze inspired layout to her station, shutting the pink and gold curtains behind her.

"Hi, I'm Dallas, nice to meet you." She introduced herself to the gentleman waiting patiently in her chair.

Standing to his feet, his skinny lanky frame towered over her, putting her in mind of a basketball player. With a head full of curly hair, his dark eyes stared Dallas up and down, clearly impressed at the sight before him.

"I'm Rico. Nice to meet you Dallas." He spoke with a set of gold teeth that aligned in his mouth.

"Rico? Ummmm… the name on your check says *Antonio*." She finally forced out as the thoughts in her head tripped her up.

Was it a coincidence that the same man who beat up and raped Trinity name was *Rico* and he was from Atlanta too? Dallas wondered if she was going crazy; it could all be one big ass coincidence, but she just had to play it cool and see.

"That's my real name." he chuckled, never taking his eyes off of her.

"Well, a pleasure meeting you, Rico. So, tell me, what we getting done today?" she asked, taking a seat on the stool in front of her supply table.

Smiling and showing off one dimple, Rico rubbed his hands together first, then through his full beard before speaking.

"Some simple shit, like, a few numbers…. Roman numbers." He spoke, displaying an empty spot on his already tatted neck.

"Ummmm okayyyyy. I usually do more complicated art and to be perfectly honest, the deposit you left is more than the worth of the tattoo. So, here's what we'll do. I'll have one of my head artists do those numbers for you. I can assure you that their work is just as good. You have my word." Dallas promised with a warm smile before standing to her, ready to redirect him.

"Nah, I don't think you understand. I only want YOU to do it." Rico replied, turning around but never leaving the spot he was in.

"And why?" she quizzed, no longer interested in playing the guessing game.

"Because I've heard nothing but great things about you. You come highly recommended." He bragged for her before taking a seat in the chair.

Saying "*fuck it'* in her head, Dallas prepped to do the work. Her day was freed up and as long as he knew he wasn't getting any change back, they were good.

"Okay so, I know you want it on your neck, but what numbers you want?" she questioned, placing the latex gloves on her hands.

Silence fell upon the room as she gathered all the things she needed. It wasn't until after a minute or so had passed that she realized he had still yet to response.

"The numbers? The numbers you want, what are they?" she asked again, ready to get the show on the road.

"Oh, a set of numbers you may know as well. I want the date August 29th, 2019. Just like the one you did for Trinity."

Dallas thoughts were confirmed, she was right. Rico was in fact Trinity's ex, but why was he on bullshit with her?

"Ohhh, so you the clown ass nigga that beat and raped my friend?" Dallas snapped, ready to square up with him off of the audacity.

"BEAT? RAPE? I choked that hoe out, but I ain't rape her." Rico barked, standing to his feet as Dallas reached for her phone.

"You a fucking lie. Yo sick ass raped her and got her pregnant and…"

Dallas's words were interrupted by Rico's obnoxious loud laughter. She couldn't believe the nerve of him at thinking that something as such was funny.

"You need to leave." Dallas yelled, pointing to the curtains behind her.

"Nah baby girl, on sum real shit. I just came for a tat and to enlighten you." Rico calmly stated, taking one step forward.

"Enlighten me on what?" Dallas questioned, taking one step back, further away from him.

"Listen, if the bitch pregnant, it ain't by me, but that's YO friend, right?" Rico paused, awaiting an answer but Dallas was confused.

"Okay, but why me? Why come fuck with me? What I gotta do with you and her?"

"You got more to do with it than you think, but Imma head out. Watch the company you keep beautiful."

Rico's rough hands rubbed the side of Dallas's face before walking completely out. Taken back by the entire ordeal, she stood there frozen, trying to figure out her next move. Rushing out of the station and to her office, Dallas packed up her belongings locking up. Giving Kia a quick rundown regarding daily operations, Dallas zoomed out the door and to her car.

"CHINKS!" She yelled aloud in the empty ride before pulling away from the curb.

"Hey Siri, call my husband."

Dallas listened as the phone rang over and over again. Calling back three more times, she slammed her fist against the sterling wheel out of frustration. He was home when she left, and according to him, he was too tired from traveling to go anywhere. Turning onto her street ten minutes later, Dallas parked behinds Chinks' car and got out. Entering through the kitchen door, she called out to him, but he never answered. Noticing his belongings on the counter, Dallas walked over and grabbed the phone next to his wallet.

"Shit. I forgot his ugly ass changed it." She quietly cursed under her breath, getting mad all over again.

Her and Chinks still hadn't had a sit-down regarding the password change because he went out of town. He's a grown man and it is his phone, however, why was he moving so differently now? Dallas needed answers.

"WRONG CODE" displayed again on his phone as she keyed in another combination of numbers.

Getting it wrong again, Dallas sat the phone down before she disabled it and really looked stupid. She planned on addressing the issue after she told Chinks about the Rico situation at the shop. The thought of his name made her feel uneasy as she wondered what role she played in it and why he wanted that same tattoo.

"August 29, 2019…. What the fuck…" she thought aloud, trying to put the pieces of the puzzle together.

The sight of Chinks's phone lightening up out the side of her eye drew her attention as a message came through. Snatching the phone up again, Dallas thoughtlessly keyed in 082919 into his phone, unlocking it.

"WHAT THE FUCK?" she mumbled to herself as she tried to figure out why her husband's password and the death of Trinity's baby coincide.

CHAPTER TWENTY-TWO

Neysa walked into Starbucks at seven o'clock on the dot and spotted Jay sitting at a table alone near the back. Using her hands to knock the wrinkles out of her blouse, she slowly walked over to him as he stood up to greet her.

"You look beautiful." He complimented, releasing her from their embrace and taking a seat.

"I don't drink this shit, so I had no clue what to order you, but…."

"Jay, I didn't come here to fraternize, but out of respect, I came here to tell you face to face that -----"

"Aw…. That's the lil ring he gave you?" Jay cockily grinned, grabbing Neysa's left hand, looking closely at her engagement ring.

Letting out a soft laugh, Neysa caught the shade, but to be honest, she thought it was cute. Outside of the playdate at Maggie's party, they hadn't spent any other time together, however, they connected so much through conversation that it was scary.

"For your information, it's a six-carat diamond cut from…."

"If you were my future wife, it'll be more like an eighteen-carat cut, but who the fuck counting?" He boasted, picking up the glass of water in front of him and tossing it back.

Rolling her eyes to the back of her head, Neysa tried her best not to blush, but Jayson was wearing her down. Dressed in a wheat colored Timberland jogging suit and boots to match, Jay rubbed her hand before she snatched it away.

"I didn't come here for this. I simply came to tell you that, although I enjoy our FRIENDSHIP, we can't continue this because I'm getting married." She finally blurted out after being interrupting before.

Neysa watched Jay sit back in the chair and smile, his reaction completely catching her off guard. In her mind, she assumed that he'll wish her well, especially seeing how they never crossed the line.

"Why you marrying that man, Neysa?" Jayson looked her square in the eyes and asked with a puzzled look on his face.

Slightly offended, she sat up straight, leaning in closer to him, so he could hear her clearly. She felt as if he was out of place for asking her that question, especially since it was obvious.

"Although it's none of your business, I love my man and…"

"You think he loves you?" Jay cut her off mid-sentence and asked, shifting the flow of the conversation.

Neysa sat, her ass glued to the chair, staring deep into his eyes, waiting for him to crack a smile or announce that he was joking, but he never did. She could tell by his posture and demeanor that he was dead ass serious, and that's what scared her.

"Yeah, my nigga loves me, any more questions?" She shot, her voice and body language full of attitude.

Feeling her phone vibrate in her pocket, Neysa broke eye contact with Jayson to retrieve it before ignoring the call from Dallas. She had every intention to call her back; she just needed to finish up with him first.

"Nah, I'll ask more questions later, it seems like you got a lot going on now anyway." Jay replied as Neysa's phone rang again.

"Won't be no later. Take care." She told him before ignoring D a second time and standing to her feet to leave.

Jayson had officially turned her off and wasted her time. She should have shot his ass a text and blocked him afterwards; instead, she wasted gas, dealing with his cocky ass.

Walking away and answering the third incoming call from Dallas, Neysa placed the phone to her ear when she felt Jay tug at the tail of her coat. Turning around, staring him up and down, and giving him the look of death, Jay released his grip and stood up.

"Trust me ma, that nigga don't love you." Jayson leaned in and whispered in her available ear.

"And won't be no wedding but you take care ma." He continued, walking away leaving her stuck, speechless for the first time.

The loud cries from Dallas in her other ear quickly snapped her out of her trance. She had been so wrapped up in Jay, and their bullshit, she hadn't heard Dallas until then.

"OH MY GOD BEST FRIEND! WHAT'S WRONG?" She said into the phone as she rushed out of Starbucks doors.

Stepping out into the winter cold, Neysa tighten the Gucci scarf around her neck while her eyes watched Jayson's Maserati zoom down the one-way street.

"What's wrong? Where you at Dallas?" Neysa questioned, directing her attention back to her best friend who continued to cry into the phone.

"I'm – I'm – I'm at your house." She struggled to get out while Neysa bussed a U-Turn in the middle of the street.

"I'm literally down the street. I'll be there in two minutes." She promised, doing forty in a twenty zone.

Pulling inside behind Dallas who sat in her driveway, Neysa jumped out the car and powerwalked over to the passenger's side of her vehicle. Pulling at the car's door, she waited for her to hit the locks before getting in.

"What happened?" she turned to her and asked, her eyes watering at the sight of her distraught best friend.

Dallas told Neysa what happened, from top to bottom, even up to the fight that took place when Chinks caught her.

"The moment I unlocked the phone, it was like he appeared out of nowhere and snatched it out of my hands." Dallas told her, pulling down the sun visor, fixing her face.

"So, you ain't get to go through nothing?" Neysa asked as she fixed the sides of Dallas's hair.

"Not a muthafuckn' thing. I unlocked that bitch and BOOM, this nigga appeared out of nowhere like a superhero." Dallas told her, causing the both of them to laugh a little.

"Okay, what happened after that?"

"I asked him why it was his code, and he tried to turn the whole thing around on me like it was my fault, and I was the bogus one for going through his shit. He hit me with the, "*if we don't have trust, we don't have nothing"* bullshit, and I spazzed out. I grabbed that bottle of Stella Rosa you left that was on the counter and tried to crack his shit, just off the strength of playing with my intelligence. We wrestled around, he choked me, and when I calmed down, I allowed him to speak.... And that's when he fucked up AGAIN!" Dallas paused, flipping the visor back up and turning to face Neysa.

"Friend, this nigga looked me in the eyes and said, "*Dallas, you ever heard of a coincidence?*" she continued in a deep voice that was supposed to be Chinks.

"So, I grabbed that statue that sits on my bookshelf because somehow by this time, we in the dining room, and I threw that bitch at his head."

"DALLAS!" Neysa yelled, covering her mouth with her right hand.

"I caught the side of his head, and he started leaking so I ran, grabbed my keys, and did the dash here." She finished up, leaving Neysa speechless for the second time that day.

"I mean… Friend, I don't know what to say." She finally got out after a few seconds of silence.

"Me either but a ***coincidence*** though?" Dallas turned her head to the side and emphasized.

"Well, unless we discover some more shit that leads us to believe elsewise, you can't go around catching domestics BFF." Neysa told her, meaning every word she spoke.

"BULLSHIT! This ain't sitting well with me and the nigga Rico was TOOOOO THIRSTY for me to find out some shit. On top of that, he says he ain't rape her…. Who the fuck or what the fuck am I supposed to believe?" Dallas rambled on and on as Neysa questioned his motives as well.

"Okay, so how about we do this? We call that nigga to get more information, seeing how he's the only person running his mouth. He told you this much, that nigga will tell you more… trust me, he sounds like a bitch ass nigga to me anyway." Neysa told her as Dallas called the cell phone number Rico left when he made the appointment.

Placing the call on speaker, both women waited as the phone rang several times before someone eventually picked up.

"Hello." A soft female's voice made Neysa and Dallas eye's buck as they stared at each other.

"Oh, I'm sorry. I was trying to contact my friend Rico." Dallas said, checking to see how she dialed the wrong number.

"No. You. You. You have the right number. Rico's my cousin, he was just shot in the head at a red light. He's DEAD!"

CHAPTER TWENTY-THREE

Trinity walked out the restroom and joined the other girls as they got comfortable in the salon's chair, preparing for their pedicure. Dallas invited her and Shonnie out for a spa day in celebration of Neysa's engagement. Stressed out more than she'll like to admit, Trinity happily accepted the invite; she was in dire need of pampering.

"So, Trinity, how far along are you now? You over there glowing and shit." Neysa said as Trini flipped through the color pallet.

"Thanks babe. I'm four months and so glad that the first trimester is over with." She replied, selecting a dark shade of green for her toes.

"I bet. I hear it's horrible." Shonnie added in, followed by Dallas's question.

"Have you heard from that fool… ummmmm… what's his name? RICO!" she quizzed; the mention of his name made Trinity feel queasy.

"Actually, he called this morning and tried to convince me to move back to Atlanta, but I cut it short and told him to never contact me again." She briefly explained.

Trinity hated talking about Rico. She hated anything that involved him; therefore, she avoided it at all cost.

Surely enough, Shonnie knew more because they were closer, and she had been there since the beginning, but a part of her felt judged whenever she spoke about it around Dallas and Neysa.

"So, the gender reveal date is set." Shonnie blurted out, changing the topic, and Trinity was thankful for that.

Cutting their eyes at each other briefly, Shonnie and Trinity shared the details regarding the ideas they've come up with thus far. Excitement spilled over as she thought about becoming a mother again. Traumatized from her last experience, Trinity knew she couldn't stress out about it much, due to the health of the baby she was carrying now.

"I think that's dope and I can't wait. I know a lady on Facebook, she's an event planner, I'll inbox her now." Dallas stated, pulling out her phone and doing as such.

Smiling from ear to ear, Trinity looked around at her circle of friends and was truly thankful for the support they were giving, especially since she had a feeling that it wouldn't last long. With the type of luck she had been having the few past years, she knew that it was just a matter of time.

"So, Trinity, I was thinking about finally letting Dallas give me a tattoo, on a scale to one to ten, how bad was the pain?" Neysa asked out the blue, shifting the conversation again.

"Girl, yo scary ass not getting nothing done. Shut up." Dallas told her, causing them to laugh aloud.

"Yes, the fuck I am. I might start of small though…. As a matter of fact, I'll get some numbers too." Neysa replied before taking a sip from the champagne glass.

"Ohhhh! I know, I'll get the dates that Ocean proposed." Neysa thought before shaking her head side to side.

"NO! That's corny. I should get something meaningful like, something pertaining my parents." She continued, lowering her head low to her chest.

This was the first time Trinity had heard Neysa speak on the death of her parents. Outside of conversations here and there with Shonnie regarding the incident, Trinity didn't know much more. Her heart ached for Neysa, but she couldn't begin to imagine the type of hurt she was going through.

"It's definitely best to get something meaningful like I did simply because you're going to have to look at it for the rest of your life." Trinity said to them as she glanced down at the tattoo on her inner wrist.

"Not to pry and I totally understand if you don't wanna talk about it but, did the doctors say what went wrong during your last pregnancy?" Trinity heard Dallas ask, snapping her out of her trance.

Looking up at all three women as they stared at her, awaiting an answer, Trinity swallowed the lump in her throat before speaking.

"Asphyxia, lack of oxygen, she was too small." She finally got out as a single tear escaped her eyes.

Talking about it, even months later, still hurt. Trinity wanted nothing more than to be a mother, but with the blessings from God, she got a second chance.

"I'm so sorry to hear that." Both Neysa and Dallas said in unison while the nail tech added another coat of polish to Trinity's toes.

"Thanks y'all, but I'm moving forward, and although this pregnancy didn't happen the way I intended it to happen, I'm still thankful."

An awkward silence fell amongst them as soft jazz music played from the speakers in the spa. The room was warm and bright, filled with flat screen TVs hanging from the ceiling like chandlers. This was her first time visiting, but Trinity planned on coming back soon.

"So, Trinity, what part of Georgia did you live in? Or were you actually in Atlanta?" Neysa asked, her eyes shifting from her phone to her.

"I lived in Duluth, it's North Georgia in Gwinnet County, but I worked in downtown Atlanta, so I traveled daily." She replied before admiring the quality work that was done on her feet.

"Word? I was looking at houses in Buford. I know that's not too far from where you were." Dallas added in as they all prepared to leave.

Reaching inside her wallet, Trinity pulled out a twenty-dollar and handed it to the nail tech for a tip.

"When? You been making plans to leave Chicago without letting me know." Shonnie said to Dallas, who placed on her shoes and coat.

"You know Chinks has a distribution shop in Lawrenceville, he always back and forth anyway, so we figured why not get a house or condo there too." Dallas said to her before sharply cutting her eyes at Trinity.

"Chinks ALWAYS back and forth. Trinity, I'm surprised you and him hadn't bumped into each other sooner." She continued.

Thanking the lady again for her services, Trinity placed her wallet back inside her purse, replacing it with her phone, which was now in her hands.

"I'm surprised I haven't either, but then again, I'm a homebody, I stay out the way." She finally replied, looking down at her phone, preparing to shoot a text.

"Thanks so much Dallas for treating us to this wonderful experience and congratulations again Neysa, we got a baby shower and a wedding to plan." Shonnie rejoiced, hugging the both of them followed by Trinity, who did the same.

Stepping out into the blistering cold, Trinity button up the gray peacoat she wore before parting ways with her friends. Quickly walking to the car, she hit the remote-control starter, warming it up before she approached. The fresh snow on the ground crushed under the gray and white Uggs she wore on her feet. Seeming like forever, Trinity finally made it across the lot and to her ride.

"SHIT!' She cursed to herself but at mother nature for her choice of weather.

"I ain't move back for this shit." She continued, just as her phone connected to Bluetooth and the voice of Summer Walker blasted through the car.

Turning down the volume, Trinity grabbed her phone to change the song as well as to shoot a text. Thinking back to the conversation she had with the ladies at the spa, she felt that something was off, and if the gut feeling she had was right, all hell was about to break loose. Always being one step ahead, Trinity did what she felt was right and that was by warning Chinks.

312-893-0089: I think yo WIFE knows.

CHAPTER TWENTY-FOUR

"Dallas, could you please get dressed so we could go?" Chinks begged from his side of the bed as Dallas watched another episode of *Power*.

She had been binge watching the show all weekend and was finally about to find out who shot Ghost when her husband interrupted her. It had been a few days since the phone and Rico incident, yet, Dallas still wasn't speaking to him. She made him sleep downstairs and kept all communication to a minimum. Whenever Chinks did try to hash things out, Dallas would bring up the password situation, and he would play dumb, pissing her off even more.

"Our dinner reservations are in less than an hour, could you get up and put on some clothes?" Chinks pleaded with her, but it went in one ear and out the other.

Chinks tried doing everything to get back in good graces with her, but Dallas refused to give in; she knew it was more to the story than the coincidence he led her to believe.

"I told you when you made those raggedy ass reservations that I wasn't going." She finally replied, turning up the volume on the tv.

They say this is a big, rich town, yeah, yeah

And I just come from the poorest part, oh

Bright lights, city life, I gotta make it

This is where it goes down, yeah (yeah, yeah)

I just happen to come up hard (come up hard)

Legal or illegal, baby, I gotta make it

Dallas sat up, preparing to rap 50 Cent's part in the theme song, when Chinks walked over to the tv, and pulled the plug out of the wall.

"I'm trying to be the adult here and work things out, but yo childish ass attitude not making the situation any better." Chinks stood in front of the blank flat screen and pleaded with his wife.

"You can call me childish or whatever fucking adjective you prefer, however, until I know the truth, I ---"

"Truth? Whose truth Dallas? Cuz I'm telling you the truth, but you are making nothing into something. Here I am, kissing yo ass for some shit I ain't do wrong. Could you please get dressed so we can talk over dinner?"

Staring straight ahead as if she could see through him, Dallas thought about her next move and what she should do about the entire situation all together. Her gut told her that it was more to the story, but she didn't know where to turn for the whole story. Rico was dead, and it was obvious that Trinity was a liar, seeing how she's still communicating with a dead man. After leaving the spa with the girls, neither Dallas nor Neysa could believe the things that came out of Trinity's mouth. The moment she stated that she spoke with Rico was the moment they knew she couldn't be trusted.

"I'll be ready in ten minutes. MOVE!" She got out the bed and said, shoving him in the chest before closing the bathroom door behind her.

If playing dumb was the only option she had in search for the facts, then playing dumb is what Dallas intended to do. What is done in the dark seems to always come to light, and it shouldn't be any different in their case.

"I'm ready, let's go."

Dallas walked down the steps in a pair of black Saint Laurent sandal heel and a fitted Fashion Nova bodycon dress to match. Keeping it simple with her jewelry, she wore a princess cut diamond bracelet along with the diamond hambone chain to match. With her eyes glued on Chinks, who sat on the couch, watching her every move.

"My wife. My wife." Chinks chanted, standing to his feet and smiling at the sight before him.

Dallas had no idea what he had planned, however, she was dressed for whatever.

"Can you hand me my trench coat from out the closet, please?" She requested, ignoring his compliments and lustful stares.

Doing what she asked, Dallas watched her husband move about, and although she was mad, she couldn't deny how sexy he looked. Blinking twice before looking away, Dallas refused to get ***dickmatized*** at a time like this. She needed to remain focus, especially if she was dealing with snakes.

The drive to her favorite restaurant, Prime and Provisions, took about twenty minutes and she was thrilled. Dallas had been craving their steak cuisine and planned on enjoying every bit of it, even it if meant ignoring Chinks the whole time. It was no secret; he knew the ways back to her heart, but this time was different; he had to come harder than a seventy-dollar plate.

"Dallas, I wanna tell you something before we walk in here." Chinks stopped her and said before she entered the restaurant.

With a raised eyebrow, Dallas looked him up and down, wondering why all of sudden, beads of sweat were trickling down his face.

"It's cold as hell out here, and we just drove all the way here without you saying a word. Whatever it is, it can wait until I'm warm." She replied, stepping around him and pulling open the glass doors.

Leaving Chinks behind, Dallas entered the restaurant and was greeted by her favorite hostess Pam.

"Right on time as usual, Mrs. Moore. Your table is ready, you can follow me, and it looks like your other two guests have already arrived."

"Other two guests?" Dallas repeated just as they stopped at a small table near the kitchen.

With her eyes finally focusing on what was in front of her, she watched as Trinity and Shonnie sat in a booth, sipping from lemon water glasses.

"What the fuck? Why they here?" she turned around and asked Chinks who stood guarded behind her.

"MARQUIS! CARE TO EXPLAIN?" Dallas spoke up again, her voice increasing with every unanswered question.

"Sit bae, I'll tell you everything."

Serving him the look of death first, Dallas then distributed it to Shonnie and Trinity, who had yet to open their mouths. Slowly taking a seat, Dallas made sure to keep her coat on, just in case dinner was cut short. Finally settling in but not getting too comfortable, Dallas looked at each and every person at the table in their eyes, yet, everyone avoided eye contact with her.

"I don't like this vibe, and if somebody don't start talking fast, Imma ----"

"I got a call a few days ago from the clinic stating that the ultrasound shows that I'm further along than what they originally thought …." Trinity paused to catch her breath, and that's when Dallas noticed the tears in her eyes.

"It turns out, Rico is *not* the one who got me pregnant… it was ***Chinks***, the night we had that threesome."

CHAPTER TWENTY-FIVE

"DALLAS, OPEN UP! I CAN HEAR YOU LAUGHING, WATCHING *MARTIN*!" Neysa yelled through the cracked window on the side of Dallas and Chink's house.

It had been almost forty-eight hours since she last spoke with her best friend. After receiving a text message a few night ago about Chinks fathering Trinity's child, Dallas powered off her phone and went M.I.A. After being ignored at the window, Neysa walked back around to the front, where she started banging on the door again.

"If you don't open up, Imma call the police, Dallas. I'm not playing with you." Neysa warned, willing to make promise with the threat.

A few seconds and curse words later, the front door came flying open, and Dallas stood with her hands on her hips, ready for war.

"Girl, go put on a wig, you look horrible. Light some candles, it stinks in here." Neysa stormed pass Dallas and complained as she opened more windows in the living room.

"When the last time Chinks been here?" Neysa looked around and asked as Dallas flopped back down on the couch.

"He ain't been back since I put him out. Told him I needed some alone time and he respected my wishes."

After finding a lighter, Neysa lit three candles from Bath and Body Works, placed them throughout the house before joining her best friend on the couch. Dressed in her favorite Spongebob scrubs, Neysa kicked off her shoes before snuggling close to Dallas.

"I thought you had to work." Dallas said to her as she pulled the cover on top of the both of them.

"I do… In an hour, but I stopped by here first since you still avoiding the world. Dallas, what happened?" Neysa sincerely asked, wanting to know the aftermath of dinner.

"They ran down the dates, it all matched up, Neysa. He didn't put on condom, we never thought about the *what ifs* afterwards. I can't be mad at nobody but myself…. that bitch pregnant by my husband." Dallas explained as tears streamed down her face.

"And Shonnie, why was she there? I called her to get answers and she never picked up." Neysa told her while wiping the tears from her eyes.

"Moral support, I guess. I mean, I get it. I just can't believe this."

Dallas cried into her hands as Neysa rubbed her back softly. She felt so sorry for her friend and wished there was something she could do to help.

"And what Chinks saying?"

"He ain't said much of nothing, other than 'he's sorry that it happened,' but how can I be mad at him when I was there too?" Dallas said, blaming herself for the mishap.

"Don't you take full responsibility for this, all parties involved were grown as fuck, and although it's a messed-up situation, it's not the end of the world. How many months is she actually?" Neysa questioned, trying her best to make her feel better.

"Five months, remember, she told us four? Well, that was before she got the results from the ultrasound. Rico ain't come around until a month later, which makes sense… it had to happen on the fourth of July."

Doing the math in her head, it all added up correctly, pinning the baby on Chinks, but now what?

"Okay, so what's next, what conclusion did y'all come to?" Neysa questioned aloud.

"I told the both of them that they needed to make the shit disappear and…"

"DALLAS! You said that to that lady, knowing how she feels about carrying a child?"

"How she feels? I don't give a fuck about how SHE feels. What about me? *I'm* his wife. The wife, who has been trying without success, to get pregnant and carry his child. Everyone wants me to think about everybody's feelings but mine." Dallas snapped, pulling the covers back and standing to her feet.

The last thing Neysa wanted to do was upset her, but things had already started to go left. It wasn't that she was siding with Trinity; she was still in shocked at the situation in whole.

"Calm down kid. I didn't come over to piss you off more. I'm simply asking, what's next? Did y'all make it to that point?" Neysa quizzed from her spot still on the couch.

"I suggested an abortion, and I don't care the cost or risk; they need to make it happen." Dallas cold-heartily replied before turning away and walking off.

Sitting there stuck, Neysa shook her head from side to side, still unable to believe how everything was playing out. Their life was like an ABC soap opera and things just continued to get more interesting with every episode.

"But why dinner though? Why he takes you out to your favorite restaurant to break that type of news to you?" Neysa yelled into the kitchen, where Dallas washed up dirty dishes.

"I wanted to know the same thing. This nigga said, because it was a safe place and he was afraid of how I'll react if he would have told me at the crib. According to Chinks, Shonnie and Trinity hit him up with the news first because neither of them knew how to come to me with it." Dallas walked out of the kitchen and told Neysa, who placed on her shoes.

The more and more Neysa listened to the story, the more questions aroused, questions that definitely needed answers.

"Okay but now, let's take it back. What about the password and tattoo coincidence? Did you bring that up? Was it any mention of that?"

"Ohhhh, you know I did and neither of their stories has changed, so I left it alone. I even thought about looking in Chinks' phone, but I know his sneaky ass ain't gon' let nun slip up." Dallas told her as she wiped her hands off on a towel rag.

"Okay look, I gotta head out for work, but I'm coming back over as soon as I get off. I'll call to see if you're hungry. I'm going to check on you during my lunch." Neysa said to her before the two embraced with a long hug.

During the drive to the hospital, Neysa reflected back on the past few months of her life and wondered how she made it to the place she was at now. In the span of summer, she loss both parents and gained a husband; however, everything seemed so unbalanced. A part of Neysa felt guilty celebrating her engagement when she was marrying the one person her parents asked her never not to. And on top of that, her closest friend was having marriage issues.

"Good morning Dr. Brown." Montana greeted her from the nurse's station the moment she exited the elevator.

Displaying a warm smile, Neysa spoke to her before joining her behind the long receptionist desk.

"What's its looking like today?" Neysa asked as she logged into the systems, preparing for the day ahead.

"Easy and breezy. Thank God." Montana rejoiced, pulling files and charts to begin her rounds.

"Dr. Shaw is on call. I'll be working the East end if you need me." Nurse Montana continued before walking away, leaving Neysa to herself.

After looking over the schedule and making a few calls, Neysa was ready for her first patient but soon found out that they were a no show. Pleased to hear that, she retreated to her office to check on Dallas, but her calls went unanswered.

"Bitch better be sleep." She said aloud, just as the phone rang back in her hands.

"Girl, cuz I was about to pull up again." Neysa answered, flopping down in the cushioned chair behind her desk.

"Pull up where?" A deep voice questioned, a voice Neysa knew for sure didn't belong to Dallas.

Removing the phone from her ear, Neysa cursed at herself for being so careless. Automatically assuming it was Dallas returning her call, when in fact it was Jayson.

"How can I help you?" she asked, rolling her eyes to the back of her head.

"It's been a few days, and I wanted to check on you. You know, make sure everything good." He replied, his voice alone making her feel some type of way.

"Like I told you at Starbucks, I'm good, and there's no need for you to call me anymore."

"Listen Neysa, we seriously need to talk, all bullshit aside and …."

Neysa could hear Jayson speaking, but she completely toned him out, her attention being on the computer that sat in front of her. Remembering Dallas saying something about Trinity seeing a doctor in her network, Neysa thought she'll do a little research herself. Doing a patient search, not only did Neysa find Trinity's file, she discovered more than she expected.

"I gotta go. Bye."

Urgently ending the call in Jay's face, Neysa went back to her call log and dialed Dallas again, this time getting an answer on the second ring.

"BITCH! YOU NOT GON' BELIEVE THIS!" Neysa said into the phone before standing up and closing her office door.

Rushing back over to the computer, she wanted to make sure she was reading Trinity's chart correctly before spilling the new tea to Dallas.

"What? What? What happened?"

"So, I have access to all patients in our network. I pulled up Trinity's chart and like they said, the bitch is definitely pregnant; however, according to this, she's ***seven*** months and not five."

CHAPTER TWENTY-SIX

Four Years Earlier

Trinity adjusted the thin straps on the yellow spaghetti-strapped dress she wore before walking out of the restaurant in Sandy Springs, Georgia. Looking around the small restaurant, she finally spotted her classmate Cindy sitting in a cozy booth near the front door. Securing the Gucci bag on her shoulders, Trinity strutted across the brightly lit room over to her.

"I came in and went straight to the restroom, I couldn't hold it. Did the waitress come over yet?" Trinity rambled on while taking a seat across from Cindy.

"Yup, but I told her to come back. You ready to start studying?" she replied, pulling out her laptop as Trinity did the same.

The both were recent graduates of Atlanta's John Marshall Law School and preparing to take the bar in the winter.

"As ready as I'm going to get." Trinity sighed, placing the prescription Chanel reading glasses on her face.

Picking up where she left off, Trinity grabbed the pink highlighter and went to work on the civil law section in her notebook. Grasping the concept, Trinity could read it back to you in her sleep, but for some reason, she still doubted herself.

"I'm going to flag down our waitress, I'll be back."

Standing to her feet, Trinity headed to the bar to request their server when she collided with a man, backing up.

"Oh shit. My bad sweetheart." He apologized the moment they came face to face.

"CHINKS?" Trinity exclaimed, squinting her eyes and turning her head to the side for a better angle.

"Well, if it isn't Miss Trinity "Thick Ass" Howard. How you been baby? I ain't seen you since high school." He noted, looking her up and down.

"It has been a while. I'm good, here with my classmate over there, studying." She replied, pointing in Cindy's direction before focusing back on Chinks.

Life had obviously been good to him from his looks, having put on a couple of pounds since school, he still looked scrumptious, and apparently, Trinity's childhood crush still existed.

"School? Word? What you in school for?" he asked, still unable to take his eyes off of her.

"Well, I actually just graduated from law school, and I'm studying to take the bar. How you been? You live here too now?"

"Nah, I do business here, so I'm always back and forth." He paused, looking behind him at a familiar face.

"Is that Ocean? Y'all still cool?" she asked, giving him a friendly smile and wave.

"Yeah, that's my bro, that nigga ain't going nowhere but check it out. Put my number in yo phone and hit me up, hopefully you can show me more of your city." Chinks flirted before calling out his number for Trinity to store.

"I'll be back next weekend. I hope I get to see you." He finished up saying, licking his full set of pink lips.

***

Trinity kept her word and contacted Chinks the following weekend and the rest was history. Two years in a relationship with Rico and things were rocky, but Trinity didn't trip much; she had Chinks flying in almost every weekend to take her mind off of him. Moving fast, the two of them fell in love and that's when shit got complicated.

Chinks was up front from the beginning about his marriage to Dallas, claiming that they were now out of the honeymoon phase and things were getting rocky. He also claimed that Trinity was his getaway, and she understood because she felt the same way about him. Things between them was going smoothly until Chinks selfishness kicked in. Demanding that she broke up with Rico, Trinity tried and tried, but he never seemed to go away. With promises of leaving Dallas, Trinity stuck around with hopes of getting her man, but she had to handle Rico first.

A few months after Trinity started working as a paralegal in a huge firm in Atlanta, she tampered with some evidence involving a case against Rico. Getting arrested but not receiving the amount of time she had hoped, Rico was out of her hair, at least temporarily. Taking a vacation one weekend and joining Chinks in Las Vegas, the couple ended up having too many drinks, which led to a night of passionate sex, resulting in the first pregnancy. Excited and overjoyed, Trinity and Chinks planned a life with the baby that didn't include Dallas. Fast forward after the still-born tragedy, Trinity tried to move on the best way she could, but it seemed impossible.

Unable to focus on the bar exam, she shamefully gave up and settled with being a paralegal. Her and Chinks seemed to be on more bad terms than good, which stressed her out as well. Sick and tired of being a side chick, she gave him an ultimatum that he didn't like very well. And then to add insult to injury, she got word that Rico was being released in less than a year. Feeling like the world around her was crashing down, she ran to the one place that made sense, Chicago.

A week after settling in her condo, Chinks showed up at her door, confessing his love for her. Catching Trinity in a weak moment, she let him in and gave in, giving him exactly what he wanted, her. It was like déjà vu. It was a repeat of what happened in Vegas, Trinity got pregnant again.

Chinks not taking the news so well this time go around, claiming that "*it was too close to home,*" hinted at her getting an abortion, but Trinity shut that shit down. She knew how it felt to carry a child and refused to give that up again, even for a nigga who is married. Realizing that she was serious, Chinks came up with another plan.

"I know you don't wanna bring Shonnie into this, but you have to, if we plan on keeping the baby. Imma invite Dallas to the club and you and Shonnie show up and y'all meet. You kick it with her a few times, and then, I'll set everything else up. We gon' tell her that you got pregnant during the threesome, but we tell her after it's too late."

"You really think that'll work, baby?" Trinity asked, slightly nervous about how things might play out.

"It ***has*** *to work. You carrying my baby, something my own wife can't do."*

CHAPTER TWENTY-SEVEN

It was like a bad dream that Dallas couldn't seem to wake up from, and no matter how far she tried to run, she couldn't escape it. There was lie after lie, and honestly at this point, she had no clue on who or what to believe. The most recent discovery, being that Trinity was seven months, took her by an even *bigger* surprise.

"You think she's lying to Chinks too? Maybe the bitch ain't get pregnant during the threesome, maybe the hoe doesn't know who her baby daddy is." Neysa yelled from the kitchen as Dallas laid across the couch.

Walking over to her with a tray of food, she shook her head from side to side before sitting up straight.

"I told you I wasn't hungry." She said to Neysa, who whipped up bacon, eggs, and toast.

"You haven't eaten in days. You been sitting around crying, throwing up, making yourself sick. Something's gotta give."

Neysa was right. Dallas had completely lost herself; she hadn't been out the house since Chinks took her to dinner. Zarkia was practically running the shop for her and her phone stayed on do not disturb, 24/7. Chinks was staying at a hotel and the only person she communicated with was Neysa.

"Well, we know one thing is for sure, that bitch Trinity is a liar. I know it's more to her than what we know, it's just a matter of finding out." Neysa stated, taking a sit next to Dallas and grabbing the remote control.

"She said Rico raped her, which I'm starting to believe was a lie too. I mean, he told me himself that he didn't. Then there's still the password situation. I refuse to let that go, but once I do crack the case, all hell gon' break loose, and if I have to beat that baby out that bitch, then so be." Dallas snapped, meaning each word that left her mouth.

"Yeah best friend, we need answers and the only person who can tell us, is dead."

Dallas and Neysa sat in silence for a few minutes, piecing the puzzles together in their head. Thoughts of calling Rico's phone again crossed her mind. Maybe his cousin could help out with more information; it wouldn't hurt.

"Who you calling?" Neysa quizzed with a raised brow the moment Dallas sprung to her feet and snatched her phone.

"Rico." She replied, placing the call on speaker as it rung over and over.

"He-Hello." The same soft female's voice answered again.

"Hey. My name Dallas and I spoke with you briefly before, the day Rico was killed and…."

"Yes, I remember you. Rico had your card in his wallet, you a tattoo artist, right?"

"Yes, Yes, I am. Rico had just left my shop the day before when he was gunned down. I had a few questions and wanted to know if maybe we can sit down and talk about a few things. Rico and I had some unfinished business to handle, and I simply need answers."

Dallas tried to sound as empathic as possible; she had no idea what she was getting into to. She didn't even know if the woman would be of any help, but it didn't hurt to try.

"Sure, Rico was my favorite cousin. I can shoot you a text with a meeting place and we can set something up for later." The woman replied, putting a much-needed smile on Dallas's face.

Ending the call, Dallas stood her feet and ran up the stairs to shower and get dressed. It was something about the tone in Rico's cousin voice that gave her hope and that's all she needed at a time like this. Slipping on a pair of gray Nike jogging pants with an oversized hoodie to match, Dallas threw her hair in a curly bun before reappearing downstairs.

"Let's go. She texted me in the shower. Grab yo keys cuz you driving."

Moving at the speed of light, Dallas made sure to lock up and set the alarm before leaving the house. Slipping on a sheet of ice, Dallas slowed down a little before she ended up in the hospital.

"Listen friend, I don't want you to let whatever this lady says discourage you anymore than you already are. I can't promise that we'll get all the answers today, but I promise you one muthafucking thing.... *We gon' get to the bottom of it.*" Neysa assured, resting her hand on Dallas's thigh before backing out of the driveway.

Different scenarios played through Dallas's head the twenty-minute drive over East. Attempting to take her mind off things, she navigated to the Google app on her phone to check her email. Since being cooped up in the house, she hadn't gone so much as far as to read a text message, let alone an email. Scrolling through the many unread messages, Dallas stopped and opened the one from her accountant. Ready to approve the finial expense report, Dallas downloaded the file to look things over, one last time.

"Okay. Okay. The meeting in New York. The tattoo convention in Florida.... A flight to Atlanta in August.... WAIT. WAIT. WAIT...I ain't travel to Atlanta last year." She paused, placing her phone in her lap as she thought about where that charge on her business card came from."

"Look, I think that's ol' girl right there." Dallas heard Neysa say, but she was too stuck to move.

"I remember. I remember. BITCH! I REMEMBER!" Dallas screamed, jumping up and down in the passenger's seat.

"LOOK! LOOK! HERE!" she continued, stuffing her phone into Neysa's face, who looked on confused.

"There's a charge on my business card for a flight to Atlanta." Dallas smiled, her long stilettoes nails pointing to her phone screen.

"Okay D, annnnddddd..." Neysa emphasized, still lost, trying to find the point she was proving.

"Chinks, bitch. It was ***Chinks***. Sometimes, he used my credit card to book flights, this one in particular being to Atlanta on August 29th. I remember it like it was yesterday. He got a call. He told me that some shit came up missing at the distribution center in Atlanta, and he had to fly out. Nigga was acting like his momma was dying, the way he took flight." Dallas paused to catch her breath, but Neysa picked up where she left off.

"That pussy ass nigga was going to see ***her***...."

"Yep! It was the day they loss THEIR baby."

CHAPTER TWENTY-EIGHT

"Neysa, I need you to grab some more scripts, as a matter of fact…."

"No, Ocean. I'm done." She cut him off mid-sentence and stated.

"No? What you mean no?" he questioned through the phone as she took a seat on the toilet.

"I'm not doing it no more. I can't keep risking my career for this shit."

"Career? Neysa, we set for life. I don't know why you even wanna work."

Neysa removed the phone from her ear and rolled her eyes before placing the call on speaker. Standing to wash her hands, Neysa headed to the sink while Ocean gave his usual speech. From the very first time she got involved, she made it clear to him that it was a one-time thing; however, as you can see, she went back on her word.

"Ocean, I worked hard all those years in medical school, for what, to supply illegal drugs to the streets so my boyfriend can run a lucrative drug cartel? I think the fuck not." Neysa paused, checking her reflection in the mirror before continuing.

"We supposed to be getting married, starting a family, and from the sounds of it, you moving in the wrong direction, and why the fuck are we even talking about this over the phone?"

Reminding Ocean of his number one rule, never conduct business over government lines, Neysa hoped that'll make him change the subject, but it didn't.

"Listen, we just need like fifty more prescription pads and then we can chill for a few months, but right now, at this very moment, I need you to grab that for me when you go back in." Ocean persistently insisted, but Neysa's mind was made up, he had to find other ways to get those pads.

"No, Ocean and I'll be home tomorrow. I'm spending the night with Dallas, bye."

"So *that's* what the fuck this is about, huh? You mad at me for their marriage issues. Like I told you when you came to me with the shit, Chinks and Dallas's relationship ain't have shit to do with me and…."

"But you knew yo dog ass friend was cheating and getting bitches pregnant!" Neysa yelled into the phone as she dried off her hands.

"I don't know what the fuck you talking about…."

"CUT THE BULLSHIT, OCEAN! Chinks is your right-hand man; you knew this nigga was living a double life and…"

"I don't know shit." He yelled, sticking to his story, which only pissed her off more.

"Listen, I know Chinks is YOUR friend, just as Dallas is MINE, so, you supposed to ride for him. HOWEVER, don't let lying for him be the reason you lose yo future wife."

Ending the call in Ocean's face, Neysa tossed the dry towel on the rack before stepping out of the hotel's bathroom. Since putting two and two together a couple of days ago, Neysa hadn't left Dallas's side. After speaking to Rico's cousin, Trish, the girls got a better angle on Trinity and honestly couldn't believe what they discovered. According to her, Rico recently got word that Trinity was the one who sent him to jail, that's why he popped up in Chicago. Trish also gave examples on how dirty and conniving Trinity was. Trish informed them that Rico told her that Trinity sent him to jail to be with a married nigga, and she knew for a fact her cousin wouldn't rape her. He *hated* her.

"You okay? I heard you and Ocean arguing in the bathroom. Everything good?" Dallas looked up from her phone and asked.

Sitting Indian style in the middle of the bed, Neysa looked at her best friend and smiled. Dallas had to be one of the strongest women she ever met in her life. Dealing with the newly discovered info, Dallas handled it like a champ, which kind of scared Neysa. Of course, she cried, fell into a deep depression, but none of that lasted long. Dallas had to have something up her sleeve.

"I don't think I wanna marry that nigga." Neysa blurted out, her words taking Dallas by surprised.

"What you mean? You and Ocean belong together." D replied, putting her phone away and giving Neysa her full attention.

"It's just that…"

"It's just what, Neysa. What?"

Walking over slowly to the bed, Neysa flopped down on the edge and buried her face into her hands. With all the bullshit, games, and drama being played in Dallas's marriage, Neysa was afraid, afraid that it may be her and Ocean's outcome as well.

"Listen BFF. Don't let my marriage discourage you. Ocean and Chinks are two different people, and just because my nigga pulled the wool over my eyes, that doesn't mean Ocean is the same way." Dallas explained as if she was reading her mind.

Neysa listened on as Dallas preached, and although she was spitting facts, something in her gut still made her feel uneasy. She knew Ocean better than anyone else, but for some reason, she felt like she was engaged to a stranger.

"Wanna know why my parents hated Ocean so much?" Neysa turned around and said out the blue, catching her off guard.

"Uhhh… He's a drug dealer, and they always wanted what was best for their daughter." Dallas sarcastically replied with a goofy look on her face.

"Duh, bitch." Neysa replied, tossing a decorative pillow at Dallas's head before continuing.

"When my mother met my stepfather, they started a college fund for me to use when I went to medical school. Since I was five, I knew I wanted to be a doctor, and they always planned ahead to make sure I was successful. After getting accepted into school, instead of using that money for what it was intended for, I gave it to Ocean so he could 'get on.'"

Seeing Dallas's mouth drop to the floor made Neysa feel ten times worse. No one outside of her parents and Ocean knew the story, and after repeating it aloud, she knew why.

"I know. I know and now…." Neysa began but stopped when Dallas raised her hand high in air.

"I heard your conversation with Ocean in the bathroom and…."

"I can explain." Neysa blurted out, quickly becoming defensive.

Neysa knew the day would come when she had to come clean to her best friend regarding the part she played inside Ocean and Chinks's organization. At a time when Dallas felt the world was against her, Neysa couldn't allow herself to keep anymore secrets from her.

"I told him today that I was done. He was on the phone pressuring me then to do it one last time, but I swear to you, I'm done." Neysa promised her with assuring eyes from across the bed.

The room grew silent as the both of them became lost in their thoughts. Neysa wondered what Dallas was thinking. Was she secretly judging her? Did she think she was a criminal? Or thief? How did she really feel now?

"I love you best friend, and we gon, get through all this bullshit, together."

Dallas leaned forward and hugged Neysa, who wrapped her arms around her as well. Life seemed to be kicking the both of their assess, but something in her told her that things were only about to get worse.

CHAPTER TWENTY-NINE

Trinity sat behind the cherry oakwood desk in her office and stared out the window, watching the snowflakes fall from the sky. Rubbing her round belly, she felt the baby kick, putting her in an even better mood.

"Come in." she yelled out to the person on the other end of the door before it came swinging open.

"What you doing here?" she looked at Chinks and questioned before he entered, closing the door behind himself.

"Why the fuck you not answering my calls?" he questioned, taking a seat in the lounge chair across from her.

Staring him directly in the eyes, Trinity knew the exact reason for the pop-up visit; she was just surprised it had taken him so long.

"I thought you was busy making up to your little wifey." She smirked, rolling her eyes and looking away.

"Don't start that shit man. That's the same little wife I had when we started fucking around and…."

"And you promised to divorce that bitch two years ago. Now if you don't mind, I have a conference call to join in ten minutes." Trinity cursed, her anger building with every moment he stayed.

She loved Chinks and hated that she put herself in the situation she was in, but now, it was too late to turn back.

"Dallas not talking to me. She changed her number. I don't know what hotel she's staying in. She ain't been home in…."

"IF YOU MISS THAT BITCH SO MUCH, GO FIND HER! WHY YOU SITTING IN MY FACE CRYING ABOUT THE NEXT HOE?!"

Fed up, Trinity could no longer mask it. She had sat around and played phony for months with her boyfriend's wife, and now, she was over it.

"What are we waiting on? She knows the truth now, and you said that was all you were waiting on. You said that was the *only* thing stopping us from being the family that we CREATED!"

Trinity gave Chinks an ear full and just like all the times before, he listened and promised to do better. It was obvious Chinks loved her too, and once Dallas was out of the way, she'll have her happily ever after.

"I'll be over later tonight after I finish up some business." He announced, standing to his feet, preparing to leave.

Walking over to Trinity, who still sat behind her desk, Chinks rubbed her round belly before placing a soft kiss on her forehead.

"Everything going to work itself out. I love y'all."

Rolling her eyes to the back of her head, Trinity waited until he was gone before joining the conference call she told him about. Forty-minutes later and a settlement out of this world, Trinity was closing her laptop, preparing to leave for the day. She was beyond tired, starving, and to top it off, her ankles were swollen. Promising her aunt that she would stop by when she got off, Trinity sent her a text, asking for a raincheck.

"I'm gone y'all. Have a good night. Be safe." Trinity yelled out to the remaining people at her firm before catching the elevator to the ground level.

Getting inside her Jag, Trinity wasted no time turning the heat on low while the car heated up. Rubbing her hands together, attempting to keep them warm, she impatiently waited before backing out of the parking spot. Making a quick stop at Walgreens to grab snacks, Trinity ran into traffic the moment she got on Lake Shore Drive. With the heat blasting and a big bag of M&Ms on the passenger's seat, Trinity listened to the rush hour mix playing on the radio to pass time. Vibing to the house music coming through her speakers, Trinity put on her own twerk show from the driver's seat. In a zone and not caring who was watching, she enjoyed the personal concert until her phone rung, cutting it short.

"Hello." She answered, not quite recognizing the unsaved number.

"Hey Trinity, this Shawn, you know the guy you hired to..."

"OKAY. OKAY. Shawn, how can I help you?" she asked, cutting him off before he said too much over the phone.

"I think I found the woman you were looking for, she's been staying at the Westin downtown. I've scoped everything out, and I can have the job done by Monday as long as you make sure that money is in my account."

"Like I told you from the beginning, money is not an issue, just make sure it's handled and the other ten thousand will be waiting for you….and don't call me back until it's done."

Hanging the phone up in his ear, Trinity turned the music up and danced even harder than before. She was proud of the moves she was making, especially since Chinks was taking his sweet little time. She had already rearranged her life too much to be with him, and if he didn't assure Dallas was out of the picture, she would.

Pulling into the parking garage of her condo twenty minutes later, Trinity killed the engine and got. Hearing laughter coming from behind her, she turned around and hit the alarm as a group of girls walked from their car. Hearing their loud obnoxious laughs made her skin crawl, but at almost eight months pregnant, everything annoyed her.

"Hey Miss! Hey Miss! You got a lighter?" one of them yelled out, but Trinity kept moving forward.

"BITCH! Don't you hear us? Do you have a lighter or nah?" She heard another voice yell out; this time, Trinity turned around.

"And while you at it, give us those keys to that Jag too." The taller one said the moment her and Trinity's eyes locked.

Realizing that they were serious, and she was out-numbered, Trinity picked up the pace, now powerwalking out of the garage towards her building doors.

"Where the fuck is building security when you need them?" she mumbled to herself as the footsteps got closer.

"Shay-Shay, get that bitch!" Trinity heard one of them yell out and that's when she took off running.

Only a few feet from the door, she tried her best to get away, but it seemed as if they were closing in on her. Running at top speed like Flo Jo to the elevator doors, God must have been on Trinity's side because they opened the moment she arrived. Jumping in, she panickily pressed the button, shutting the elevator doors in their face. Bending over, completely out of breath, Trinity tried to think of her next move.

"COPS!" she said aloud, preparing to call them to file a report when she noticed her phone no longer in her hands.

"FUCCKKKKKK!" She screamed out in frustration, realizing she dropped it running from those hoodrats.

CHAPTER THIRTY

"Ma, thought you said that you stopped eating pork?" Dallas looked across the kitchen table at her mother Justine and frowned.

"I tried baby, but Oliva over here won't stop bringing the shit in the house." Her mom replied, blaming her mother O.

Dallas's eyes shifted back and forth between the two before slowly handing them the pack of bacon out the fridge.

"I just want grits. Y'all can keep the swine, I'm good." She turned up her face and shrugged before slamming the refrigerator doors shut.

Popping up, surprising them that morning, Dallas pulled them out of the bed, begging them to cook breakfast. It had almost been a month since she's last been home, and she craved nothing more than a hot cooked meal.

"You over there slimming down a little too much. Everything ok?" Oliva eyed her daughter and asked as Dallas looked on puzzled.

"Ummmm yeah. You know I work out and unlike y'all… I stopped eating that bullshit." She cursed, jumping back to avoid getting slapped by Justine.

"Nah, I know a stress diet versus a healthy diet when I see one." Oliva continued, knowing her only daughter far too well.

Leaning against the sink, Dallas took a sip from the glass of orange juice in her hands and decided to remain quiet. She knew there was no use in lying to her moms, so she decided to come clean.

"I stopped over here to see y'all, but I got a meeting with my lawyers downtown."

"Meeting for what?" Justine questioned as she poured coffee into her favorite sunflower mug.

"I'm divorcing Chinks." She nonchalantly replied, pulling out the wooden chair in the kitchen and popping a squat.

"WHAT?" They both yelled out in union as Olivia, the dramatic one, acted as if she was having a heart attack.

"Yeah, I found out he's been basically living a double life, one here and one in Atlanta." She paused, laughing to herself.

"Ma, the nigga even brung the bitch to Chicago, had me befriend her, and…."

"Where this bitch at? Where this nigga at?" Justine, the gangster mom, jumped to her feet and yelled as she pulled her shoulder length dreads into a ponytail.

"Ma. Calm down. I promise it's not that deep." Dallas explained, but it wasn't enough to control her.

"Why are you so calm baby? Are you sure you okay?" Oliva questioned as she reached over, rubbing Dallas's hand.

"I wasn't but then I realized crying ain't gon' solve shit. What happened, the things that took place.... could never be erased. I been sitting in a hotel room, contemplating suicide when that nigga was probably somewhere getting his dick sucked."

That was a plus with having two moms, they understood and never judged. Justine and Oliva have always been Dallas's best friends, and she loved them dearly.

"What is he saying?" Justine asked, finally settling back down in her chair.

"We have our first face to face today and..."

"Wait baby, you going to see your lawyers BEFORE even talking to your husband face to face." Her mom quizzed, the both of them wearing the same puzzled look on their faces.

"Yup, cuz ain't shit Chinks can say that'll make me stay." Dallas proudly declared before standing to her feet, answering the front door.

"You expecting somebody?" Both women asked their daughter, who simply shook her head yes before disappearing from the kitchen.

Walking through her parents' house, Dallas's heart smiled at all the memories from her childhood that lingered there. Some of those memories being good and others not so good; however, life was less complicated then, and she missed that.

"COUSSSIIIINNNNNN!!" Dallas pulled the door open and yelled as the hawk entered her mother's home.

"Hey Favorite. I missed you." Shay Shay smiled before hugging Dallas and stepping in out of the cold.

"Yo aunties cooking, you want a plate?" Dallas offered, the smell of turkey sausage filling the air.

"Nah, I can't stay long. My ride double parked. I just stopped by to give you this." Shay Shay replied, going inside her pocket and pulling out an iphone Max.

"That pregnant bitch must've ran track cause she got outta there fast." Shay continued, causing Dallas to laugh.

"As a matter of fact, that hoe did run track in high school." She noted before examining the phone and realizing it wasn't locked.

"You know me and my girls can beat the baby out that bitch next time if you want us to. We'll make sure she can't run." Shay wickedly stated as she turned to leave.

"Nah, this phone good enough. You know us women NEVER erase shit. Good looking out cousin… I'm going to Cash App you when I get back to my phone." Dallas told her before closing the door and stuffing Trinity's phone in her pocket.

"That sounded like Shay Shay." Oliva reported the moment Dallas re-entered the kitchen.

"It was, she was brining me something. Is the food almost ready, I'm starving?"

Changing the subject so they wouldn't ask any more questions, she grabbed a bowl, preparing to make a fruit tray. Dallas knew her parents weren't done asking questions; however, she didn't plan on telling them, EVERYTHING.

"So, this meeting, where is it taking place?" Justine started back up and like she thought, it was only a matter of time.

"We are meeting at a public place. I told him he had fifteen minutes to say whatever it is that he had to say." Dallas informed them before dropping a slice of orange in her mimosa.

She meant it too. Chinks hurt her to a point of no return, but she refused to be damaged; therefore, she needed some type of closure.

"I just wanna know the basics like, why?"

"Why? HMPH! Baby, you'll never get an answer that is good enough to justify the hurt he has caused you. Now, I can't lie, I've always loved Chinks like a son, and everyone knows he loves you too, but what he did was foul…. and…. what about the lil hoe he was cheating with? Where she at?" Justine rambled on and that's when Dallas decided to end it.

"She's around, I guess. I haven't heard or seen from her though. Even Shonnie, she been MIA too, and both me and Neysa been calling her. Honestly at this point, I need to take care of my mental health first, and I'll worry about dragging those bitches later."

Having heard enough, both Justine and Oliva shook their heads up and down, smiling, like the proud parents they were. Even Dallas was shocking herself, the way she was going about handling things. Maybe it was an age thing, growth is real, and Chinks and Trinity had God to thank for that.

"Okay ma, I'm about to go. Thanks for breakfast." Dallas said, kissing Oliva on the cheek first before hugging Justine, who started washing dishes.

"You're welcome and we love you, baby."

"Right and call us when you make it to the restaurant and the moment you leave. As a matter of fact, drop your location just in case." Justine rounded out saying, causing Dallas to laugh as she headed to the front door.

"I LOVE Y'ALL!" She yelled out to them before closing the door and stepping onto the porch.

Running across the snow filled grass to her car, she got in, plugged up her phone, and searched the restaurant she was meeting Chinks at. Dallas thought long and hard about this meeting. At first, being one hundred percent against it, but after realizing she needed it more so for herself, she agreed.

Driving less than five miles, Dallas pulled into the packed parking lot, lucking up on a spot not far from the door. Noticing the time, granted she was a few minutes late; however, she still didn't see Chinks's car.

"Double life having ass bastard probably got a whole car I don't know about either." She cursed, pulling out her phone and checking the email he sent.

After changing her phone number and not being able to get a hold of her, Chinks started emailing, and that was his only means to contact her. With everything being correct, Dallas sat back and waited for him to arrive. Growing impatient after ten minutes and no sign of him, Dallas started her car back up and prepared to pull out when her phone rung. With not many people having her new number, her mind instantly began to wonder who could be calling.

"Hey girl, hey!" D sang into the phone after realizing it was nobody other than Neysa calling.

"Dallas, where you at?" her frantic voice alerted her as she merged into traffic.

"Leaving from Oakbrook. I was supposed to meet Chinks there, but he never showed up. What's up?" she questioned, getting annoyed as she thought about how he wasted her time.

"I just got off the phone with Lou… he said Chinks just got picked up by the FEDS."

CHAPTER THIRTY-ONE

As soon as Neysa ended the call with Dallas, a gang of red and blue lights swarmed her car. Looking out her rearview mirror, she squinted her eyes to see who they were after when she noticed them surrounding her car.

"What the fuck!" she cursed aloud as officers in both squad and unmarked cars jumped out pointing their guns.

"Neysa Brown." An older white man with a gray beard, dressed in blue jeans, hoodie, and a bullet proof vest barked after yanking open her car door.

"Yes." Neysa hesitantly replied, her heart racing and her mind wondering.

"I have a warrant for your arrest, come with me." He continued, pulling her out of the car and placing handcuffs around her wrist.

Completely in a daze, Neysa sat in the back of a Chicago Police Department squad vehicle with her eyes closed and her head hung low. Her mouth dry, she couldn't form a sentence to even begin to ask questions, so she sat back and cried until they arrived at the station.

"Put her in room two. I'll be back." The same arresting officer said to a young Asian cop before walking off towards a set of stairs.

Stumbling forward, Neysa tripped over her shoestring as the young man tried to help her catch her balance. Yanking away from him, he laughed aloud before shoving her in a room and flicking on the lights.

"Have a seat." He ordered before slamming the door shut.

Flopping down on the cold steel chair, Neysa buried her face in her hands and cried before quickly sitting up and wiping her eyes.

"I ain't did shit." She said to herself, remembering all the episodes of the *First 48* she has watched.

Tears was the first sign of guilt, and if her thoughts were right, she had to act innocent, even if she wasn't.

Feeling her phone vibrate in her pocket, Neysa wondered if she should grab it or not. She hadn't been searched or even processed, but she needed to at least let Ocean know what was happening. Thinking about it too long, the second she reached for it, the door swung up.

"Ms. Brown. Ms. Brown." Jay walked in cockily and smiled, almost making Neysa fall out of her chair.

Strolling around her slowly as if he was taunting her, Jay finally stopped and took a seat in the chair directly across from her.

"Listen, Imma cut this on." Jay began, holding a silver and black tape recorder in his hand.

"And when I do, every question I ask you, you reply with, *'I want my lawyer.'*" He said, pressing the button and getting down to business.

"Ms. Brown, I am Federal Agent Jayson Bishop, how are you?" Jay said, causing Neysa's mouth to fly open wide.

"Do you know why we brought you in today, Ms. Brown?" Jay continued, moving his head up and down slowly, motioning for her to play along.

"I -I -I want my lawyer." She stuttered while he smiled before continuing.

"We've got word that you have connections with the Midwest Drug Cartel." Jayson stated and that's when Neysa felt her world crashing down.

"Ms. Brown, is that true?" he urged, discreetly grabbing her hand from across the table and rubbing it.

"I WANT MY LAYWER!"

Neysa looked Jayson in the eyes and yanked her hand away; she couldn't believe what was happening to her, nothing seemed real.

"That's all the questions I have." Jay replied, winking his eye at her and cutting off the tape recorder.

Staring at each other for the next minute or so, neither of them spoke and the more she looked at him, the more her curiosity grew.

"I'm sorry and I have no business even explaining this to you, but I ***have*** to." Jay paused, grabbing her hand again, pulling it closer to his.

"Listen to me and listen to me good. Ocean has been working for the FEDS as a mole for the past year. We got video of him murdering a man a few years back, and in exchange for a lesser sentence and charge, he's been snitching on everyone in his organization, including you and Chinks."

"Wait. Wa- What?"

"Baby listen, he's been trying to get you to do one more job, right?" Jay asked as Neysa shook her head up and down confirming.

"The FEDS gave him until last night to turn in that as final evidence, but because you didn't go through with it, he lost out. Now, they've built enough to take down all the big shots like Ocean, Chinks, Monte, and Von, but you, you Neysa, you still have time."

Hearing Jayson talk turned Neysa's stomach; it literally made her sick. She couldn't believe the man that she's sacrificed so much for was willing to take her down, for his own gain.

"They planning to raid your crib. When we release you, go straight there and destroy anything that may incriminate you. Do the same with your office. I'm about to tell them to let you go." He finished up by saying.

Standing to his feet and grabbing the tape recorder, Neysa grabbed him by the arm, stopping him before he left.

"But why? Why you doing all this?" She looked up at him with teary eyes and asked.

"I like you Neysa, a lot." He smiled, showing off the dimples she loved.

"When I ran into you at the hospital, I knew who you were, but I fucked up when I brung my daughter into it. Kayla's crazy about you, and one night, she told me that you reminded her of her mother, and I thought about it, she was right. I see more than a bad bitch when I look at you. I see someone caring, nurturing, funny, and innocent."

Tears fell from her eyes, but just like before, she quickly wiped them away. Sitting alone for another five minutes before being released, Neysa reflected on life and why hers turned out the way it did. Grabbing her phone to call an Uber, Neysa broke down crying the moment she unlocked it. Her screensaver, a picture of her parents, stared at her, forcing her to remember how they were the first ones to see the signs. Wanting to call and apologize but the fact that she couldn't ate away at her the most. Neysa sat there, staring at the picture, wishing she could hear their voice one last time.

"OH MY GOD!" She wept, remembering the day they died and how they called her back to back, but she was too busy working to simply pick up the phone.

Feeling like the worst daughter in the world, Neysa navigated through her apps when she remembered a voicemail they left, but she never checked it. It was too soon after their deaths and she couldn't handle hearing their voice, but in the present, that's all she wanted to hear.

"Hey Neysa, this is Amy from Comcast, please give us a return call at…."

Skipping through the unnecessary ones, Neysa stopped when the recording read the date, letting her know she reached the right one.

"Neysa, this is Dad. My friend Judge Ford called me today with some disturbing news. Please call me back…."

"Neysa, this is Dad again. I'm at the shop now and you still not answering any of our calls, but hurry up and call back, it's an emergency."

Neysa's heart skipped a beat. Each time a recording ended and another one began, she could sense in her father's voice that something seriously was wrong.

"Neysa…. Neysa…. It's me and your mom and we are…."

Neysa placed her ear closer to the phone, trying to make out the noise in the background as her father struggled to speak.

"It's --- Ocean ---- he's ----"

POP! POP! POP! POP!

The sound of four loud gun shots echoed through her ears before the recording ended.

CHAPTER THIRTY-TWO

"Just sign here for me and you have a nice day." The Mexican Value City employee said in broken English as he handed Trinity the clipboard.

Signing on the line, she thanked him again before shutting and locking the door behind him. Looking around her new place, she smiled; things were finally starting to come together, and her house was looking more like a home.

"Whew, chile!" She hissed as another Braxton Hicks contraction caused her to bend over in pain.

They had been coming back to back that day when she usually only got them at night. With only two weeks until her due date, she knew she could go into labor at any moment, but she was prepared.

Walking bare foot on the shiny hardwood floors, Trinity entered the baby's room and smiled, admiring the neutral colors throughout. A part of her was still nervous, thinking about the outcome of delivery, but there was nothing she could do but pray. She tried her best not to stress out, but there was so many things to stress over. Heading back down the hall, the sound of her ringing phone made her change directions. Cutting on the bedroom light, Trinity's eyes searched the room, landing on the nightstand where the phone was located. Grinning from ear to ear, recognizing the number, she quickly answered.

"You have a call from an imamate in a Federal Correctional Facility……"

Wasting no time, Trinity interrupted the robot and pressed one to accept the call.

"What's up, baby?" Chinks's voice said from the other side, widening the smile on her fat face.

"Finally got a new phone, I see. How you been?" he continued, the noise in his background increasing.

Turning up the volume up on the phone, Trinity laid back on the bed and spoke from the heart.

"I miss you so much baby, and I swear to God I'm working my ass off to get you out of there. Those charges are some bullshit, and I know that the partners at my firm have what it takes to win your case." Trinity babbled on and on while Chinks listened quietly.

When he got locked up, she didn't know what to do. She thought it was some type of joke when his friend called her with the news. What took her for an even bigger shock was when she learned Ocean was the one who gave them away.

"Listen, I don't want you stressing about me and you got a lot to deal with in the real world. Make sure my baby is good and healthy and then we'll work on me coming home." He told her as the first set of salty tears escaped from her eyes.

Absolutely nothing was going as planned and that's what frustrated her more than anything else. Her and Chinks thought long and hard about their plans to be together, only for it all to come crashing down.

"Ummmm... Trinity." She heard him call her name, snapping her out of the temporarily trance she was in.

"Have you --- Have you heard from Dallas? I mean, Shonnie say anything about her? She's been posting on Facebook?" he asked, his question making her pull the phone from her ear and look at the screen.

"Excuse me?" She sat up and replied, trying to make sure she heard him right.

"Nevermind, man. I ----"

"The nerve of you to ask me about that bitch when I'm the one carrying your child, or did you forget that? I'm the one crying at night, wondering how I can rebuild my life, rebuild a life, for you.... For us." She sobbed, her emotions getting the best of her.

"Trinity listen, all I was saying was...."

"FUCK YOU!" She spat, ending the call in his ear and tossing the phone on the side of her.

Laying on her side in the fetal position, Trinity cried herself to sleep, hoping that by the time she woke up, the bad dream would be over. Sleeping for about an hour, the loud sound of her doorbell ringing made her pop up. Looking over at the time on the cable box, it was ten minutes after seven, but the dark room made it feel so much later.

"I'm coming, I'm coming." She yelled down the long hallway towards the glass front door at Shonnie, who pranced around the front porch.

"Hey bitchhhhhhhh!" Trinity sang the moment she pulled the door open.

"Big momma. Look at you. How you feeling?" Shonnie asked before the two embraced with a huge hug.

"Like shit but you look good." Trini laughed as the two of them entered the warm home.

Trinity gave Shonnie a tour of her new place, and she loved every bit of the two-story house. Discussing home décor ideas at the kitchen table turned into an all-night thing, but Trinity was thankful, thankful that she had someone help keep her mind off of Chinks.

"Shonnie, I wanna apologize for pulling you in this bullshit. I know you said---"

"It's cool, you can't help who fall in love with, and----"

"But you loss two friends behind my relationship and that's not cool."

Shonnie knew from the beginning about Trinity and Chinks, from the moment they met at the coffee spot. Yes, she was friends with Dallas and Neysa, but Shonnie made it clear that her loyalty was always with Trinity. Thankful for her and her friendship, Trinity still felt bad for dragging her in it.

"And if they feeling some type of way about me, we all grown women, they'll have to find a way to resolve it." Shonnie ended with, and Trinity left it alone at that.

Relocating to the living room to watch a movie, Trinity grabbed a bag of popcorn to put in the microwave while Shonnie prepared the beverages. Ripping open the plastic bag, Trinity felt something pop. Rubbing her stomach, she looked down when she felt something wet, and lo and behold, she was leaking, her water bag bussed.

"SHONNNIIIIEEEEEEEEE!" She yelled out from the same spot as if she was afraid to move.

Rushing over, Shonnie opened her mouth to ask what was wrong when she noticed the gray leggings, she was wearing was wet.

"Bitch. I didn't come over for this!" She looked at her and said before rushing back over to the couch to grab her phone.

"Should we call an ambulance?" she panickily asked, but instead, Trinity shook her head no.

"The baby's bag is packed on the rocking chair in the room and my overnight bag is next to it. Grab my keys, I'll grab a towel……let's go!"

The two women moved about the house doing what was required of them. A feeling of excitement took over as she thought about what was happening. The time had come, and God had given her another chance to be a mother.

"Aight, I'm ready." Trinity announced from the door as Shonnie walked her way with two bags and purse.

"I'll call my auntie from the car. This baby feels like it's coming nowwwww." She grunted, holding the lower part of her belly.

Seeing the fear in Shonnie's eyes tickled Trinity as she tried to be less dramatic as possible, but she was truly in pain. The contractions were getting closer and closer, and she wasn't sure how much longer she could take it. She debated back and forth with herself regarding natural labor, but the way she was feeling, she needed strong meds, STAT!

"The hospital up the street. Hang in there, friend." Shonnie encouraged from the driver's side as they headed to Northwestern Hospital.

A ten-minute drive turned into five minutes as Shonnie did the dash on the expressway. Thankful for her, Trinity wondered how she would have gotten through this, if she was alone at home.

"I'll go get someone. Stay put."

Jumping out the car, Shonnie flagged down two employees, who rushed over with a wheelchair and rolled Trinity in.

"It feels like I gotta shit.... Oh My God!"

"That means the baby is ready, we'll get you into a delivery room ASAP. Morris, can you take this patient to room nine while I call her mid-wife? Start prepping her, I got a feeling this baby doesn't want to wait."

Hearing the nurse slightly calmed Trinity down, but she knew the worst part had yet to come, and that's what she was dreading most. Entering the room, the hospital crew worked fast to get her set of for labor, but according to the baby in her stomach, they weren't moving fast enough.

"Lay back, let me check you." A woman dressed in light blue smocks with a set of blonde curl rods came in and said to Trinity.

Laying back, Trinity opened her legs wide as she could, but the pain she was experiencing was becoming unbearable.

"I need an epidural." She cried out, hoping that someone would answer her prays.

"No time, I see a head full of hair already. Now, I'm going to count to three and you push until I tell you to stop. Okay?" The woman looked up at Trinity and directed with a warm smile that made her feel much better.

"Okay, one.... two.... three.... PUSH!"

"STOP!"

"You are doing an awesome job. As a matter of fact, one more big push like the first one and your little bundle of joy will be here…. one… two… three…. PUSHHHHHH!"

Pushing with all her might, Trinity closed her eyes, giving the best she had when the sound of a baby's cry erupted in the room.

"Good job mommy, and congratulations, it's a boy!"

Tears of joy flooded her face as she held her baby in her arms. The feeling she felt was unexplainable and his chubby yellow face made it all worth it.

"You got a name mommy?" the doctor asked as they cleaned her up and allowed the two time to bond.

"Yup. Marquis. He's a JR."

Everything after that moment was a blur, but everything she went through to get to that moment was a well worth sacrifice. She was obsessed with MJ and even more because he looked just like his dad. Nothing in the world could take that joy from Trinity, well, at least she thought.

"I'm going to take MJ for a while, but he'll be back once we evaluate him. In the meantime, get some rest and again, congratulations!"

Hesitantly, Trinity handed off MJ to the hospital crew before being left alone. Looking around the room for her phone, Trinity remembered Shonnie having it, so she decided to buzz the nurse's station and request for it.

"Damn, that was fast." She said to herself the moment she ended the call and the hospital room doors swung open.

Sitting up slightly, Trinity smiled as she waited for Shonnie to enter; however, her smile quickly turned into a frown when she noticed a team of cops entering instead.

"Ms. Trinity Howard. You are under arrest for the murder of Antonio Rico Walker. Cuff her to the bed."

CHAPTER THIRTY-THREE

Two Years Later

"Ms. Townsend, here's the keys and congratulations, it has been a pleasure doing business with you." Thomas, her relator, said before handing over the keys to her new tattoo shop.

"Thank you so much for making my dreams come true." She yawed, grabbing them from him, and in return, she gave a firm handshake.

Looking around at the empty space, Dallas admired the layout and couldn't wait to put the finishing touches on it. Shop two was in full effect, and she couldn't have picked a better location for it.

Stepping out into the Texas heat, Dallas looked around the parking lot of the strip mall where her new spot was location and beamed because all her dreams were finally coming true. Stepping off the curb, she hit the locks on her black Tesla and got in. Bringing her new baby to life, Dallas rolled down the windows before turning the air conditioner on low. Checking the rear camera placed inside the dashboard, she carefully backed out and headed home.

It had been a year since she made the move from the Midwest to the South, and she didn't regret it one bit.

She loved Chicago to death, but the saying was true, everything was bigger in Texas. Turning up the radio and blasting Megan Thee Stallion, Dallas twerked in the cream leather seats, cruising down the highway. Reaching her exit ten minutes later, D snagged a park in front of her condo building and got out. Reaching for her purse, she felt her phone vibrating inside the bag and retrieved it, laughing at the silly picture on front.

"Hey girl. Heyyyyyyy!" Dallas sang into the phone before getting out the car.

"Hey bitchhhhhh! I thought you was gon' be here this weekend. What the fuck happened?" Neysa cursed from the other end, causing D to giggle.

"It's next weekend and don't be acting like you thirsty to see me when you barely answer the phone."

The hardest part about living in Houston was being away from her parents and best friend. She missed Neysa so much, and although they didn't talk on the phone every day, they made sure to make time when it was needed.

"I was just telling Jay that yo ass was gon' blame it on me." She cursed, Dallas hearing the happiness in his voice.

"Tell my brother and TT baby Kayla I said hey. I'll call you back, my other line." Dallas told her before rolling her eyes and clicking over.

"You have a call from an inmate in a Federal Correctional Facility……"

Selecting the option for yes, Dallas kicked off her red bottoms and flopped down on the gray and pink furniture inside her living room.

"Da- Dallas. What's up, baby?" Chinks's voice rang out as Dallas placed the call on speaker.

"What, Chinks?"

"How you been? I'm surprised you answered. I knew you still loved me." He gloated; the sound of his voice made her want to vomit.

"I only answered because I heard your grandmother passed away, and the least I could do was give you my condolences, and now that is done, BYE!" she shared before looking down at the Rolex on her arm.

"DALLAS! DALLAS! WAIT!" Chinks called out before she ended the call.

Remaining silent, Dallas gave him the opportunity to speak, and that's exactly what he did.

"I know I fucked up, and although we aren't legally married anymore, I still love you, want you, and need you in my life. Ghee, you were the best thing that happened to me. All I ask is that you give us time...."

"TIME? HMPH! Nigga, the only person that has ***time*** *is you. Enjoy that life sentence homie, bye."*

The day Dallas confiscated Trinity's phone, she ran across the text message between Trinity and Chinks, where they spoke about killing Rico. Turning that into the cops landed the both of them doing time behind his murder. Last Dallas heard, Trinity's son was being raised by her aunt, but either way, she didn't care. Ocean ended up being killed in prison six months back, but everybody seen that coming because no one likes snitches, especially niggas in jail. He deserved that and more after what he did. On top of being a rat, he killed Neysa's parents. Neysa's father's friend, who's a Judge, got wind of the case against her, and instead of warning her first, they confronted Ocean, which resulted with their lives being taken. He never wanted them to tell Neysa, so Ocean took matters into his own hands.

If you had asked Dallas ten years ago how her life would turn out, she never imagined it being the way it was. But if she had to do it all over again, in the end, she would. The lies, secrets, and betrayals made her a better woman while that cheating ass bastard Chinks made her a richer one.

You see, Dallas and Chinks both agreed to a prenup, one of which included an infidelity clause. The reason Chinks was so bent on making Dallas believe the baby was conceived during a threesome was because he knew she could take EVERYTHING if he ever got caught.

Buzz. Buzz. Buzz.

Standing to her feet, Dallas adjusted the Gucci traps on her tank top and headed over to the door to answer it. She knew exactly who it was, and yet somehow, butterflies still formed in her stomach. Snatching the door open wide, Dallas stared at Junior, who stared back at her. Feeling her pussy throb, Dallas licked her lips before grabbing him by his full beard, pulling him inside her place, and he couldn't do anything but laugh at her antics. Junior had been helping Dallas out a lot, especially when he let her sit on his face.

THE muthafuckn' END

Made in United States
Orlando, FL
10 November 2024